The Patsy

The Patsy

Robert Gambogi

Other Novels by Robert Gambogi

Revolution
A Proper Life
Right of Survivorship
The Woman In The White Cellar
Right of Survivorship
Young Mr. Watson
Leaving Cuba
Searching For Home
Darkness All The Way Down

Poetry Collection

Love and Other Psychotic States

Screenplay

Right of Survivorship

1

The sound of the tapping on the loose pebble glass of my office door mixed in with my dream—a little woodpecker pecking on a white skull in the desert to get at the dried-up brains inside.

I was asleep on my office couch and in no mood for whoever was at the door.

The tapping continued. "No one here!" I yelled.

The tapping kept up. I threw my legs to the floor and waited for the small of my back to ease up, then stood and tried to stretch. "Hold your damn horses," I called out and started my way across the room. Halfway there something walloped my right ankle. I bent down and picked up the empty quart bottle that had once held nearly a day's supply of Old Overholt rye whiskey and dropped it with a clang into the tin wastebasket by the desk.

There was more tapping at my door. When I got there I fumbled with the lock until I remembered that it was broken. I opened the door.

Her mousy hair was pulled back with a vengeance. She looked out at me through large thick-lensed cheap plastic-framed glasses that gave her eyes a startled look.

She stood staring, her mouth making little movements as if she was trying to recite something that she couldn't quite bring to memory. "Yeah?" I said.

She kept staring, her mouth still now.

"Can I do something for you?"

She clutched her long red scarf. "You're in your. . . . You're only wearing your underwear," she finally got out.

I looked down. Fortunately, it was my clean boxer shorts and a tee-shirt with only one small hole.

"Wait there," I said, closing the door.

My pants and tie and shirt were in a heap next to the couch. I went and put them on.

At the small sink in the corner, I threw water at my face, then looked into the cracked mirror above the crusty sink bowl. "Not good," I said to the reflection.

I checked my zipper as I went back to the door.

She was still standing there. "Sorry," I said. "It's so early. Caught me off guard."

She stared at me. "Early?"

I stared back. "Okay, what time is it?"

"Past noon," she said.

"Well . . . Einstein," I said.

"Einstein?"

"All time is relative to the observer."

She blinked twice, then said timidly, "I'm looking for Mr. Frank Malory. The detective."

"All right. It appears you've found what's left of him."

"I have come to hire you, Mr. Malory," she said with a little more firmness.

"Come in, come in," I said. "We can't conduct business out in the hallway."□

She took a step across the threshold, looked around quickly and came to a stop. I looked around also, getting a visitor's eye view of the place. I felt sorry for the occupant. "You'll have to excuse things, I've been too depressed to do any housework since Reagan got elected." Dropping into my chair, I pointed to the client's chair. She hesitated a moment longer, then decided to take the plunge and came the rest of the way in and took a seat. □

"Now, what is it you need and how much money do you have to get it?"

"I would like you to find my brother," she said in her frail voice.

"Your brother."

"Yes," she said. "You do that, don't you? Find people?"

I stared at her. She didn't wear any makeup as far as I could tell, her features flat and undefined, signs of age creeping in. But if you looked, you soon saw there was a delicateness of bone structure, a balance of line and curve under nice skin that could be appealing. Underneath all that plainness was quite possibly a handsome woman. Her eyes were a muddy brown, though something made me think they should be blue. Her nose was very straight and proper as if wrought by design. Her lips, though pale, were quite nice. □

"You're making me nervous staring at me like that," she said, turning her head to the side, flushing a little.

"Tell me about this missing brother."

She kept her head turned. "He's not missing. We were separated when we were young. Our mother and father divorced. I went with Mother and he went with him."

"I see," I said when she didn't add any more.

She turned to me. "And now I want to find him. You can understand that, can't you?"

I nodded.

I pulled open the middle drawer and searched for cigarettes and found an unopened pack. Carefully peeling the little red tear strip, I wondered when they'd start another scam about saving them. It had probably been more than twenty years since I'd heard any more of that deal.

"Mother died soon after the divorce. I was raised by my aunt. My aunt Rachael."

I scratched around inside the drawer for a working Bic. Rachael, I thought, now there's a name you don't hear much anymore. The third lighter I tried spouted a tiny flame. I rushed the cigarette tip to it.

"My father didn't even come to the funeral. I never heard from him or my brother again after Mother's death."

I saw a rainy day long ago, a lot of cheaply dressed people gathered around a cheap pine coffin, a kid in a house dress and big glasses and no makeup standing next to the coffin as it got lowered into the ground. I couldn't see even the trace of a tear in her big blue eyes.

"Now I've come into a small inheritance, and I want to use the money to find my brother."

Probably poor Aunt Rachael. I bet she hadn't cried at that funeral either.

"You were recommended to me," she said.

I blew smoke. "Who?"

"By this man." She carefully reached into the black plastic purse that had been sitting in her lap and took out a business card and held it out toward me. "He said he used to work with you."

I leaned forward and took the card. "So he's a lieutenant now," I said.

"He told me to give you his regards."

"Harvey Moss and I were on the force together here in San Francisco, but he's in L.A. now."

"I live in Los Angeles."

I handed her back the card.

"The last I had heard of them, my brother and father were living in San Francisco. That's why I wanted the recommendation of a detective here."

"Makes sense," I said.

"I know that doesn't necessarily mean he's still here. By now he could have moved to anywhere. But I have to start somewhere, don't I?"

I nodded.

She looked at me, the big eyes behind the big glasses getting a little filmy. "Is there a possibility you could find him for me?"

I shrugged. "If a person doesn't care if he's found, it's pretty easy to find him. There's a lot of trails running to all of us. On the other hand, if a person doesn't want to be found, and he knows how to get himself lost—well, that's a different story altogether."

"Yes, I can see what you mean." She took a handkerchief from her cheap purse and dabbed at her eyes. "Perhaps I shouldn't even try. Maybe it will only make things worse for me if he can't be found at all."

"Maybe," I said. The handkerchief looked oddly expensive, maybe embroidered silk.

She fixed her glasses and straightened up in the chair. "No, I'm not going to turn back now. I want you to find him for me."

"You do?"

She looked at me questioningly. "You doubt me?"

"You haven't asked how much it will cost."

"But I told you, I have some money from an inheritance."

"How do you know it will be enough?"

"What would be the price of it?" she said haltingly.

A strange way to put it, I thought. As if she weren't used to asking how much things cost. "Like I said, it could be easy, which won't cost much, or it could be hard, which *will* cost much."

"Whatever it is, I'm prepared to pay it."

"Okay. Sounds fine by me. Now, do you have any reason to believe your brother might not want to be found?"□

She looked away again. "From what little I have heard, Orin turned out— Well . . . kind of wild."

"Wild?"

"I believe there have been instances with the authorities. He may even have spent time in jail."

"That could make him easier to find."

"Perhaps he is in jail now. I don't know."

"That would make him very easy to find."

"Even if he were in jail, even if it were for something very bad, I would still want to find him."

"I understand," I said.

She looked me straight in the eye. "Do you have any brothers or sisters, Mr. Malory?"

"I've got a brother in Des Moines. He's a doctor back there. I don't think I'd pay to see him, though. But that's another story. I get what you mean."

"Do you?" she said. There was sternness in her voice now, like she was talking about something that really mattered to her. "I don't know what your brother did to make you feel that way, but at least you had the opportunity to dislike him. I have only this lacking inside. This question. We judge ourselves by our family, you know." She brought the handkerchief out again and dabbed at her eyes. "I can't say it in so many words. But I will never rest until I am reunited with Orin, even if it's only for a few minutes."

I stubbed out my cigarette and took a notepad from the middle desk drawer. "If you want me to work full time on your case, which I suppose you do, it will cost two hundred dollars a day plus any expenses above the normal cab fares, postage, phone, etc. I'll need five days in advance, a thousand dollars, as a retainer and you won't receive an itemized list of the expenses, just a total." She nodded as she opened her purse and brought out a lump of folded bills. I watched as she carefully counted out the retainer then stuffed the rest back into her purse. It looked like she had expected to pay more, but in my condition I was in no position to press it.

"His name is Orin Hammond," she said. "He was older than I. We were so young when we were split up that I couldn't really tell you what age he is now. He was my older brother, that's all I can tell you about him."

"Do you want a receipt?" I said as I wrote the brother's name on the notepad.

"I don't feel that would be necessary."

I slipped the bills into the middle drawer. "You said you had heard he was in San Francisco. Who'd you hear that from?"

"From my aunt."

"Where did *she* hear it from?"

"I don't know."

"What exactly did she say?"

"I don't know what you mean."

"Did she just lower her paper at the breakfast table one morning and say 'Your brother's in San Francisco,' and then went back to her sports page?"

She carefully smiled. "I see what you mean. It

was about eight years ago. We were talking about my father. She didn't like my father. She was saying it was too bad that Orin had to go with him. She said she had heard that Orin had been picked up by the police. In San Francisco. Something about dirty movies, I think. That was the end of it. I didn't ask her any questions."

"I see," I said, making notes. "Is it possible that your aunt knew more about his whereabouts than you thought? Did you ever ask her where you could find him?"

"She always said it was better for me never to see him. Anyway, she has passed away." She placed a hand on her scarf and squeezed it gently.

"And you've tried the obvious, like looking in the phone book."

"Yes. I've telephoned every Hammond in the Bay Area."

"Give me your address."

"Can't you just call me when you find him? My number is two-one-three area code, five-nine-one-seven-six-three-five."

"You don't want a written report?"

"No."

That was strange. But at that moment she was a gift horse and I didn't feel like counting teeth. "All right."

"But I don't want him to know I am the person looking for him. Can you do that?"

"If you want me to."

"I just don't want him to know I am looking for him."

"Okay."

She smiled that careful smile again, the upper lip rising just to the gum line, so only teeth showed—the way a Miss America contestant would smile. "I feel better now," she said and gave another little squeeze on her scarf.

"Good," I said.

"Well . . ." she said in her taut little voice. She stared at me, half at me and half over my head, as if there was something moving on the wall behind me. "I guess I have things started."

She snapped the purse shut and half looked at me once more, then gave me another of the careful smiles and got up. She started to turn, then stopped. She extended her hand over the desk. "It was nice meeting you, Mr. Malory. I hope you will find Orin soon."

I stood up and took her hand. She must have had a very warm heart. "I hope so too."

She took her hand back and straightened her coat, then turned and went out the door.

When she had gone, I sat back down and pulled open the side drawer to take out a glass and the nearly empty pint of Old Overholt.

I downed a drink, then took the bills out of the middle drawer and set them gently on the desk before me. I felt like I was stealing her money; it would be a very simple investigation. But then, how much is a brother worth?

2

There were only a few customers scattered about when I entered Eddy's, the hangout not far from my office frequented by the Mission Precinct where I had once worked and anyone who liked good jazz without the hassle of tourists. At the far end, the little narrow stage was lit but no one was playing yet. The place only holds about a dozen tables, little ones with just enough room for drinks, and four chairs clustered tightly around. The walls were black, the ceiling blacker, the lighting dim and smoky and the floor was worn soft pine. In front of the small stage was a little polished wood dance floor. Along one wall running from the door and halfway to the stage was the bar with Eddy standing behind it polishing a glass.□

He looked up as I took my usual stool at the far end from the door. "Mistah Malory." He put the glass on the counter and threw the white towel over his shoulder with a snap, then reached down nimbly and took out a bottle of Glenlivet Single

Malt from under the bar and poured the glass he had been working on and shoved it to me.

"How've you been, Eddy?" I said.

"Just great. Just great indeedy. You missed a good month for music down here," he said, leaning on one elbow against the bar. "Yes sir, missed some fine music. But important thing is you seem to have crawled outa your hole."

"I've got a new client who left me enough retainer to pay my bills and eat for a while."

His smile faded. "You gotta get over it, my man. Can't let a thing like that get you down. That woman flat out lied to you."

"The world's full of liars. That's what I'm supposed to figure out, Eddy. The lies from the truth."

"Man can't always do what he's 'sposed to do. Best if he can do it most 'tha time."

"I'm supposed to protect people, not get them killed."

"You didn't get that woman killed, man. No way. And what about me? Year ago guy in here pulls a piece on me and says he's gonna blow me away 'cause I'm too black. Shoots a damn thirty-eight slug that runs right by my head then draws the hammer back for another try. You and that big piece flew him right off his stool before he could do me."

"I was just lucky to be here at the right time."

"Ain't no luck, man. You a guy what knows what has to be done and stands up and does it. Not a lot a guys like that left."

I took a sip from the drink, then got out my wallet and laid down money on the bar.

"Don't have to pay the whole thing all at once. I never wanted your piece for no collateral anyway. Just thought it better with me than anywhere you could lay a hand on it you was so messed up."

"I like to keep my accounts clean. Life's easier that way."

"Yes, indeedy," he said.

He took the bill from the bar. "Yes, indeedy," he repeated, the last word sailing off with a high pitched laugh as he faded into the smoky darkness at the other end of the bar. There was a burst of light, then darkness again. He had gone into his office. Another burst of light and he reappeared. "Back in a flash with the stash," he said and thumped a crumpled brown paper sack onto the bar.

Eddy was too tall to have been a jockey, but he'd never have qualified for anything more than towel boy on a basketball team. His hair was mostly salt dashed with a little pepper and tightly kinked. He had skin the color of imported dark cordovan shoes. Everyone liked Eddy, you couldn't help it.

I looked around to see if anyone was watching, then pulled the Colt .45 automatic out of the paper sack, and slipped it into the leather holster strapped below my armpit.

He said, "I took a close look before puttin' it into the safe. Gave me a funny feelin' when I was holdin' it. That's the piece you used, right?"

"Yeah."

"Like I said, felt funny to be holdin' the thing saved my life that night."

"Yeah, guns. I hate guns."

"I know what you mean, but I tell ya, I'm in love with that baby."

We both laughed. I put a bill on the counter. "What's that?" Eddy said. "You buyin' drinks for the house?"

"Interest," I said.

He dropped his lids halfway over his bright eyes, furrowed his brow, and said, "Ain't no interest, man. You ain't gonna make me take interest. No sir, ain't gonna take no damn interest."

I picked up the bill and shoved it into my coat pocket and said, "You're a tough man to do business with, Eddy Brown."

A hand squeezed my shoulder and I twisted to see who it was. "Parmeter," I said.

"Where you been Frank?"

"Nowhere," I said for lack of a better answer to give him.

"Been nice not having you bother me."

"Well, I need to bother you one more time. Need a name run."

He was a short balding man who ran the records at the Mission Precinct. Occasionally I'd been able to have him do some computer runs for me.

"Sorry, Frank. We got orders not to waste computer time on square badges. Besides you still owe me twenty for the last one."

I took out my wallet. "Here's fifty. Name is

Orin Hammond, last known whereabouts here in San Francisco, may have once done a rap for vice."

Parmeter looked down at the money on the bar. "Advance payment. Things must be looking up for you, Frank." He scooped up the bills. "I'll call you tomorrow."

"Not too early," I said.

He nodded and moved on to a table where some other guys from the precinct had gathered.

I drank down the rest of my drink, then swung around and looked out over the room. A young couple got up from their table and walked arm-in-arm to the jukebox. He put in a bunch of quarters and she started pushing buttons. It was a jukebox Phil Elwood would kill for, a museum of ancient '78's. Lester Young came out playing "Lady Be Good," and the couple moved on to the little dance floor.

Eddy leaned his elbows on the bar and propped his head on his hands, and the two of us watched the dancers like we'd never seen anyone dance before.

Eddy poured and I sipped from my drink and we listened to Lester Young's solo. I thought about how much a genius could put into a childishly simple tune of three chords and a basic two-beat rhythm.

The door opened and I turned to look.

I slid from the stool and crossed to the door, getting there as it was swinging shut. By the time I was outside, she was disappearing into the fog.

I called out her name. She ignored me. I ran up

the sidewalk after her. "Sam," I called again from only a few feet behind her and she stopped. She stood rigid. "Why did you run off?"

"I don't want to talk, all right? I was just stopping by for a few minutes after work. I saw you and left. Let's leave it at that, all right?" She stared down at the sidewalk.

"You come to Eddy's by yourself?"

"I told you, I was just stopping by after work." She still wouldn't look at me.

"I'll walk you to your car. This isn't a great neighborhood to be out in after dark."

She put up a hand as if to stave me off. "Frank, I'm all right. I can get to my car myself. Go back."

It had been a little over three months since we'd called it off. I had regretted our decision almost immediately, but she wouldn't let me reach her, even had her phone shut off. Then I'd gone into hibernation over the disaster of the Gorson case. I couldn't figure why, after all that hiding from me she'd ended up coming into Eddy's tonight.

She looked different, harder, more tense than I'd ever seen her. Even her auburn hair looked tense in the flashes of pink light from Eddy's neon sign. She had always been willowy, but now she looked like she was trying to be a model on a magazine cover.

I put my arm across her shoulders and started us walking up the sidewalk. "Come on," I said gently. "I'll take you to your car."

She walked with me, keeping her head down.

"Have you been all right, Frank?" she asked after we had walked about a block.

"I've been fine."

"No, really, I've been worried."

"I'm okay," I said.

I felt her shudder a little and knew she was starting to cry. I always made her cry.

"Godammit, Frank, why do you do this to me?" she said, taking a handkerchief from the pocket of her long black coat.

"Just a knack, I guess," I said and pulled her tighter against me.

We walked on and she sniffled and blew her nose, then put her arm around my waist and leaned her head against my shoulder. "Where's your car?" I asked.

"We passed it about two blocks back."

We kept on walking. The wind had picked up, the fog blowing thicker. Cars rumbled past us, and we were greeted with colorful epithets. A beer can flew at us from a low-rider Chevy whose tail nearly dragged the pavement, but I didn't care—I was happy walking along Mission Street through the fog after dark with Sam under my arm.

The tossed beer can must have broken the spell for her. She stopped and straightened up and gave her nose a final blow, then stuffed the handkerchief back in her pocket. "Let's walk back to my car before you have to shoot somebody," she said.

We turned and headed back. When we got to her car, it wasn't the old white Volkswagen Bug convertible; it was a black Mercedes. "You got a new car," I said as she fumbled in her pocket for keys.

She stopped fumbling, and for the first time looked up at me. I watched the flashes of pink from the sign reflect in her filmy, brown eyes. "Let's go back inside. You can buy me a drink," she said.

I followed her into Eddy's, trying to figure out what I'd said that had suddenly changed her mind. She didn't head for our regular table right off the stage where we used to sit with the music beating into our heads and sweaty dancers flying around us while we made love with our eyes across the tiny table.

We had been an odd couple. She was from a moneyed society family, had been to Eastern finishing schools and had married a handsome prince from the right family, which turned into ten years of an abusive husband who then ran off with his secretary, leaving Sam broken and confused and wondering what to do now that the fairytale had finally died completely. She'd wandered Europe for a year or so, feeling sorry for herself, then dragged back home and ended up enrolling in USF extension law school. Three and a half years later she graduated near the top of her class.

We had met while she was serving as a paralegal for a crummy lawyer I sometimes did work for. God only knows why, but Sam and I had hit it off. She was a lot younger than me and a lot prettier, but we fell in love anyway—beauty and the beast.

Like a cat trying to live with a dog, I used to say about us. But it had worked—for a while. She liked jazz and I showed her what the real stuff was.

It was six months of sex and happiness.

Maybe it was just too much, the beauty of our life together. Who knows how these things go. She was nervous and high strung. I was loose and sloppy. Like I said, we called it quits and she went into hiding.

Back inside Eddy's, I held a chair for her, then went up to the bar, and Eddy poured us two Glenlivets.□

I placed the drinks on the table and sat across from her. "Here's to us," I said. She didn't pick up her glass. I held mine out in the air waiting for the toast that never came.

"Okay," I said, "here's to us from me."

"Frank, I'm married now," she said, looking me straight in the eye.

I had tossed back half the glass of Scotch, and it lay on my tongue like battery acid. I swallowed to keep from spitting it out. It burned all the way down my throat and around my stomach. I felt my face draining. My fingers on the glass tightened until I had to force them to let up.

"I'm sorry, Frank," she said.

I put the glass down and it thumped twice on the table before I was able to let it go. "Congratulations," I said."

"I wanted to tell you first, Frank, but, dammit, I couldn't find you."

She looked at me the way you look at a horse

you have to shoot. "You didn't have to tell me first," I said.

"I wanted to. I didn't want you hearing about it from someone else."

"Who's the lucky guy?"

She looked away. "Terry," she said softly.

"Terry Gardner?"

"Frank, I don't want to talk about it, alright?"

"Okay," I said and drank the rest of my Scotch.

"I don't want you making cracks about him. We're married and that's it. He treats me just fine."

"Okay."

She took a gulp of her drink and looked up at the empty stage. "He loves me. He's nice to me. I'm a junior partner in his firm now."

"What happened to the consumer law you were going to practice?"

"I still spend time at the co-op."

"Jesus, you know, I can't figure why the hell you'd marry Gardner? He's a bigger asshole than your first husband. What did you go through the divorce and law school and everything for? You only ended up where you started. You didn't get anywhere at all."

She shot up, the chair falling over behind her. "I'm leaving," she said and headed for the door. I let her go.☐

I sat and stared at nothing for a long time, telling myself I had no justification for feeling disappointed in other people. Still, it got to me when I saw a waste. Sam was just starting to become something. She had gotten free from the pampered rich-girl trap. She had been starting to see and feel, to come alive.

I picked up the two glasses from the table and brought them to the bar. Eddy poured me another Scotch. "She's married," I told him.

He nodded. "She started coming 'round here 'bout a week ago," he said. "Started askin' 'bout you—if I'd seen you or heard from you."

"Yeah?" I said.

"Yeah," he said. "She said she was worried 'bout you. But I think it's more'n that. I think she's worried 'bout herself, too. I think she thinks maybe she done a stupid thing marryin' that man. I think that's one very confused lady."

"I think you're right," I said and pushed my empty glass toward him.

He refilled my drink and did so several more times until I went stumbling back to my office a little after two a.m.

3

My eyes snapped open, then roamed the world outside. I was in the office. It was daylight, close to mid-day, judging by the shadows through the window. I was on the couch still in my clothes that clung to me by a layer of cold sweat. My mouth felt parched and blistery. I tried to throw my feet to the floor and sit up, but my lower back became locked in a sharp pain, so I decided to go back to sleep.

My eyes popped open again. Something was waiting to chase me, and I was too tired to run from it anymore.

I got my feet carefully to the floor one at a time and hoisted myself into a sitting position, wondering if this was how old people felt in the morning.

I found half a pack of cigarettes in one jacket pocket, a working Bic in the other, lit up and pulled dry smoke into my dry mouth. I coughed.

When I was finally on my feet, I hobbled to the little cracked mirror above the sink. What I saw wasn't good. It was wrong to be in this condition when I had a case. Somebody was paying me too much money to do a job I wasn't doing.

The building my office was in had once been converted to a rooming house and there was still a shower in the bathroom at the end of the hall. I got soap and razor and towel out of my bottom desk drawer and marched myself off to get cleaned up.

Scraped and scrubbed, I didn't look so bad. I still had the suit Sam and I had bought in Las Vegas—dark blue, almost black. I had only worn it once, the night of my big win at the dice tables. Most of my wardrobe was stuffed in the bottom drawer of the green file cabinet, waiting till there was money to send it out.

There was still a shirt fresh from the laundry. I worked on a tie with some lighter fluid. There weren't any clean socks, so I took a pair to the bathroom and squirted hand soap inside them, then placed them over the nozzle of the shower, hosing them out with a torrent of hot water.

I draped the socks over the electric heater in my office and turned the switch to high, then took polish and brush to my cordovan wing tips.

I dabbed on some of the Aramis that Sam had given me on my birthday, ran a brush through my hair, put on the warm socks, and tied my shoes with even bows.□

Not bad, I mused examining the transformation.

I took a stiff hit of rye, just to say farewell, then locked the bottle and glass in the green file cabinet.

I sat at my desk and took out the notes on the Orin Hammond case:

Last known whereabouts, San Francisco.

Possible scrapes with the police.

Maybe in the porno rackets.

Mid-forties?

No description, because the last time my client had seen him he'd been a kid.

End of file. I squeaked back in the chair, lighting up a cigarette. Not much to go on, but I had solved cases with less of a head start.

The phone rang; I picked it up: it was Parmeter. I had forgotten about talking to him last night.

"I'm over at Eddy's," he said in a hushed voice. "Like I told you, they're really clamping down on using precinct computing time for anything but official work."

"Getting harder and harder for a cop to make a dishonest dollar," I said.

"You say it, man. Got a pencil ready?"

"Yeah."

"This was easy, you probably could have found him yourself in the phone book if you'd looked. You were right, several minor beefs. Peddling salacious material to minors, stuff like that. What looks like a current address is two-eighteen Steiner here in the City. Guy doesn't appear to be hiding out from anyone, can't see why you're involved."

"That's all I need. Thanks, Parmeter."

"Yeah, sure. Don't bother me again, Frank."

He hung up

4

It was threatening heavy rain when the cab left me off in front of the Casablanca Apartments on Steiner, one of those two-story, cheaply built, singles complexes in the form of a horseshoe with a big pool surrounded by scraggly palms in the center. Even though it was cold and about to rain, half a dozen girls in bikinis sat around the edge of the pool, their legs dangling in the water.

I walked up the concrete stairs and went down the outside corridor to two-eighteen, knocked, and waited. No one came. I heard music inside and knocked again. The door opened a few inches. "What!" she said with menace.

She was short with straight waist-length blond hair and dull gray eyes. I guessed her to be a little over twenty. She had on a white terrycloth bathrobe and was in bare feet like she had just stepped out of the shower. But her hair wasn't wet and she had a drink in her hand.

"I'm looking for Orin Hammond," I said.

A little sneer came to her lips and her lids narrowed like a cat's whose fur has been rubbed the wrong way. "What do you want that shit for?"

"Does he still live here?"

She looked me up and down. "You a cop?

"A private detective," I told her. "I'm trying to find Orin Hammond."

"Does that mean he's in trouble?"

"No."

"You going to punch him in the nose and break his legs if you find him?"

"No."

"That's too bad."

"Oh?" I said.

"Yeah, somebody should punch him in the nose and break his legs. Somebody should be real mean to the shit, 'cause that's what *he* is—real mean."

"He doesn't live here any more, then?"

She took a long, slow drink, her dull eyes staring at me over the rim of the glass the whole time. Then she stepped back, threw the door open with a bang and turned to go inside. "Come on in. I'm lonely anyway. And you don't look like a mean guy."

I followed her into the living room. Expensive looking men's jackets and slacks and shirts were strewn about, severely ripped as if someone had taken a butcher knife to them. I stepped on something and looked down. It was a butcher knife. A boom box in the corner was playing some kind of New Age music. The only furniture was a couch that looked expensive, very Italian-modern in light mauve leather. It looked out of place in the messy room.

She sat down on one end of the couch. There was a large white Persian cat on the other end. She patted her lap and said, "Come on, Bert," and the cat pranced to her and dove in. She stroked him and took a sip from her drink. "Sit down," she said.

I sat down where the cat had been. She held her glass out toward me. "Want a drink? It's Stoli. I've only got one unbroken glass left, but we can share." I shook my head. "Oh, like a cop," she said.

"What?"

"Like a cop. You don't drink on duty."

"That's right. Like a cop."

"So why aren't you going to bust up Orin if you find him?"

"I've only been hired to locate him."

"Who'd pay to find Orin? Most people I know would pay to get rid of him."

"When's the last time you saw him?"

She smiled coyly and went back to stroking the cat, and said, "You're not big on foreplay are you."

"I don't want to take up too much of your time."

"Oh, I've got plenty of time—oodles and oodles."

She downed her drink, then sprang up from the couch. The cat tried to hold on to the terry cloth but couldn't and fell to the floor with a thump. Apparently not all cats always land on their feet.

I heard her throwing ice cubes into the glass in the kitchen; then there was the sound of pouring. When she came back, the tall glass was nearly full. She leaned over me and held the glass an inch from my face. "Sure you don't want just a little taste?" she said with a giggle.

I couldn't help but notice she'd rearranged the bathrobe while she was in the kitchen, it was very loosely tied now.

I refused the drink and looked her in the eye with a cold look that told her I refused the rest, too. She stood up and squeezed the top of her robe tight together around her neck.

She sat down on the couch with a plop, like she'd been dropped from the ceiling. The cat ran to her and made a leap for her lap but she swung her hand out and knocked him on his back again. "That Orin's a bastard. If I pay you will you knock his lights off?"

"I don't do that sort of thing."

She looked at me. "You're big enough to knock his lights off."

"That doesn't give me the right."

"Orin's no small guy, but you're bigger and you look a lot stronger. You're older than him, but you still look real strong."

That dreamy look was coming over her again. The cat took another try at her lap and she let him land. I asked, "Have you got any idea where I could find Orin?"

"As far as I care I hope he's in Alaska freezing his balls off."

"Is he?" I asked.

She laughed. "No, he's not in Alaska freezing his balls off. I just wish he was. He's probably out at the bay, breaking some other poor dumb broad's heart."

She drank nearly half the glass of vodka in two big swallows, then burped softly. She started stroking the cat. She picked him up and hugged him to her face, then kissed him on the nose and set him back in her lap.

I took out my pack of cigarettes and offered her one. She shook her head. "Mind if I do?" She shook her head again.

I knew a lot about heavy drinkers from first hand and I could see she was nearing that stage where you get real close to your core self just before falling off into oblivion. "That what he did to you? Broke your heart?" I asked in a soft voice as I exhaled smoke.

She nodded. Tears started spilling. "He said he loved me. Said he'd always stay with me. He gave me pills, said it would make us better lovers. We fucked out at the beach house and he said it was the greatest fuck he'd ever had." The tears rolled off her smooth cheeks and fell on the cat's ears, which twitched with each tear. "He said it was me and him forever. A week later you could watch us fucking for fifty cents in the back room of any porno store in the Tenderloin."

"You didn't know he was filming you?"

"Him and his fucking hidden cameras. Shit, I didn't know anything."

I looked around for an ashtray and didn't find one. I got up and went to the kitchen to get rid of my cigarette.

There was nothing left of the kitchen—literally:

no refrigerator, no stove, no oven, a hole in the countertop where the sink had been. There was a half-full quart bottle of Stolichnaya vodka and two empty ones and a bag of mostly melted ice on the counter. I dropped my cigarette into one of the empties.

I turned to go back to the living room but froze in the doorway. She held a snub-nosed .38 police special pointed right at my chest. I couldn't tell if the hammer was back, it's really hard to focus on anything except that nasty, black Cyclops eye about to spit a hole in you. I looked at her eyes, to see if they had murderous intent. I couldn't tell, they were fuzzy and vague and hardly looking at me at all.

"He said I was the prettiest girl he'd ever made it with," she said in a dreamy tone. "He said he loved my tits, that they were full and firm and he loved the feel of them. He said he loved my thin waist and tight ass. He said I was the best lay he'd ever had."

While she talked I advanced, real slow and cautious, almost no perceptible movement at all. I figured I needed to be within thirty-six inches to take a swipe at the gun with my right foot while I kept my arms and hands stock still. If I threw the kick fast enough I'd be okay; even if she went for the shot, by the time it got off the line of fire would be over my head. It could be done and I'd done it before. Only I'd been younger and a lot quicker then.

"He was full of shit," she went on. "I told him

to get his ass out of here. I didn't care if it was his place. I told him to just get going. I've been living here ever since I threw him out. I've been selling his things to live on. I sold the sink yesterday. Got twenty-five bucks for it. That'll teach him to let people see me fucking. For turning me into one of his porno whores. And if he tries to come back again and throw me out, I'm going to put a bullet through his eyes."

I felt I was in range and shifted my weight slowly and carefully to my left foot.

"I'll put a bullet in his crotch. I'll shove this gun up his ass and shoot his brains out." She laughed, then tossed the gun to me. "You're a smart guy, look and see if I got that thing loaded right. The guy at the store I bought it from wouldn't load it for me, said I had to take it home and do it myself. Sit down and light up another cigarette and have some Stoli and see if the fucking bullets are in alright. I probably got them in backwards. Orin comes through the door and, *bang*, I shoot my brains out because I got the bullets in backwards. Then who's the dumb shit?"

I sagged with relief. I popped open the cylinder and there they were, six little fat shiny brass .38 shells. She had the cat in both hands and was pressing his face against her lips, gurgling little cooing sounds. I took the opportunity to relieve the gun of its shells. I laid the emasculated weapon on the couch, slipping the shells into my coat pocket. She put the cat back in her lap and turned to me. "Well, how'd I do? Did I get them all in straight?"

"Yeah, you got them in real straight," I told her.

"Good, I want be ready for the shit when he shows up."

"And what if he doesn't show up?"

I could tell she was having difficulty focusing on the world outside. She squinted and looked real hard at me. "What d'ya mean?" she said thickly.

If I was going to get anything out of her it was going to have to be quick. "Maybe I should go tell Orin you're looking for him. Tell him to come around and see you."

A smile slowly drew across her face. She downed the rest of her drink and got up. She stood wobbling in front of me. "You just wait here, Mr. Private Detective Man. I'll go get us another drink and we'll talk."

She tottered determinedly into the kitchen. This time there was no sound of ice, just vodka pouring.

She came back with subtlety thrown to the wind—the white tie of the robe hanging loosely at her sides. Holding the front of her robe pinched closed at her waist, she shoved the full glass of vodka at me and I took it. She giggled and went to the corner of the room where the boom box hummed its soulless synthesized music. She popped out the tape and tossed it aside, then worked hard at inserting another one. Finally she got it in and Frank Sinatra started asking for someone to fly him to the moon.

She swirled around in a graceful motion that was surprising, considering her condition. The robe spread out. She set up on her left foot and took another swirl in the opposite direction, spinning the robe open wide. I had to agree with Orin, she did have firm full breasts, a nice thin waist and a tight behind.

Oh the pity of it all, I told myself, that such physical perfection should be wasted on the young. She came and stood in front of me. "Well?" she said with a breathy giggle. "You going to dance with me or not?"

I set the glass on the floor and put my arm around her and took her hand and we started dancing through the empty living room.

I thought about all the strange circumstances I had fallen into during my career as a detective and I couldn't come up with one as bizarre as this, dancing with a nearly naked, barely post-adolescent girl in the middle of the afternoon in a mostly vacant apartment. Ah well, Malory, I told myself, if you were twenty years younger you might make something of the situation. As it was, my main concern was trying not to step on her bare toes.

The tape must have been something she'd put together—when Frank finished going to the moon it switched to a Bossa Nova.

As though she'd been trained in a Skinner box, at the first sound of the new rhythms, she pushed me away and began dancing on her own. The robe dropped to the edges of her shoulders and she gave a bump and a shrug and it fell to the floor.

"Sit down and have your drink and enjoy the show," she said, throwing her head back with a laugh. "Most people have to pay money for this, but you can have it for free because I'm bored today."

I dropped to the couch and lit a cigarette and watched. Despite her condition, she was performing pretty well, moving with a sensuous grace. She must have had some background in modern dance. "Is that where you met Orin?" I said.

"What do you keep talking about that shit for?" she said as she turned and gracefully bent over backwards with her arms snaking the air above her in rhythm to the beat.

"I want to find the guy and send him up here so you can blow his brains out."

"Blow his balls off, that's what I'll do to the big shit."

She began twirling in furious turns, her hair and breasts flying out from her body. "Where were you dancing when he met you?" I asked.

"At the Orion Club," she said from inside her twirl. "Fridays and Saturdays. He paid a hundred bucks for a private performance in the back room."

"Does he hang out there? At the Orion Club?" I asked as she twirled past me.

She began to wobble, like a top running down. The smile faded and she slowed unsteadily. Her last turn carried her legs around uncontrollably and she fell to a sitting position against the wall, her head hitting with a thump, like a watermelon hitting the pavement.

She looked for me, each eye seaming to search in a different direction. One of them found me, while the other one kept looking. She held out a limp arm. "I'm tired of dancing," she said. "Let's fuck now."

"Sure," I said, getting up from the couch. "I thought you'd never ask."

She held out her other arm. I knelt and looked into her pupils and felt the back of her head. I didn't think the bang against the wall had done her any serious harm. It was just the drink taking its final toll and delivering her into the oblivion she craved.

She wrapped her noodle-like arms around my neck as best she could and puckered her lips and closed her eyes. I did give her a quick kiss, just for sweet dreams.

She went limp under my kiss and I took her up in my arms and went down the hall with her to the bedroom.

Besides the litter of shredded men's clothes on the floor, there was only a brass lamp with no shade and a mattress with one blanket. I lowered her carefully to the mattress and covered her with the blanket.

I gave her one last kiss for good measure, then left the apartment, locking the door behind me.

5

When I left the apartment, it still hadn't rained. But the sky was very dark. Darkness at noon, I thought, looking up at the stillborn clouds—a sky full of ill omen. My grandfather who'd been a farmer up in the Valley of the Moon would have said it would be a day on the farm when the milk wouldn't taste so good and the butter wouldn't churn and the eggs would be laid cracked.

I turned up my collar and walked to the bus stop.

Back at my office I sat and smoked for a long time and stared at the green file cabinet. It probably wasn't smart to stop drinking too abruptly, I told myself. Could be hard on the heart. Still, it felt good to prove that I didn't have a problem.

I turned in my chair and looked out the window. The world looked dreary on both sides of the glass.

A plump bluebottle fly who had been pirouetting through the heavy air of the office landed on the window and watched outside with me—a proud creature, reveling in its green iridescence, free from sin, never killer only thief. I wondered where flies went when it rained, the ones who weren't lucky enough to have a dry and warm detective's office to hang out in. They probably crawled under the dumpsters behind French restaurants and played around in the drippings from last night's escargot and rack of lamb.

I lit another cigarette and blew smoke at the window. The insect on the glass took offense and sailed back into the air of the office, doing a couple of figure eights, then disappearing to do whatever it is flies do when they're not flying.

I intended to go to the Orion Club and see if I could find Orin Hammond, but it was only late afternoon and, even if the place was open, the regulars wouldn't be gathered yet. There was nothing to do until at least ten o'clock.

There were things I could do. I could write up the report on the guy I had been following because his wife suspected he was bisexual and was afraid she was going to catch AIDS. But why? Her retainer check had bounced and she wouldn't return my calls. She'd probably decided to forget the whole thing and become a lesbian.

No, out of the myriad things I could do on a gloomy afternoon, the only one that made any sense would be to sit back with a bottle and wait for the rain. But I wasn't drinking today, so I wasn't going to do that. So I had nothing to do, so I turned in my chair and stubbed out my cigarette and let my eyes drift close.

The knock wakened me. I looked up as the door opened. There was a tall busty blond looking down at me with iridescent green eyes. She was wearing a flame red Cashmere jogging suit with a pleasingly deep V-neck top, her hair pulled back like she'd just come from the gym. She was mature but athletic and beautiful and had on Chanel No. 5.

"Your secretary wasn't in the outer office and your door was unlocked, so I knocked and came in," she said.

I rubbed my eyes then looked up at her. "Yeah, well I fell asleep here at my desk. The rain, you know."

She looked at me funny. "Rain?"

I turned in my chair and looked out. The sun shone bright and the sky was delphinium blue. Somebody had washed the window—maybe that's all that had been needed. "I thought it had been raining," I said.

She settled gracefully into the soft maroon leather client's chair, taking a deep breath and wiping the back of her hand across her forehead. "I've just come from my workout," she said with a bright smile. "I must look awful with my hair back and no makeup."

That meant that she had naturally long lashes and naturally red lips and naturally blushed cheeks. Could be. "What can I do for you?"

"My name is Melanie Sturgis," she said and smiled again like the smile was part of her name. "I need someone to find my brother."□

Not another one. "Your brother?"

"We had a falling out many years ago. And now my uncle—well, our uncle, really—has died and left everything to him, to my brother."

"What's everything?"

"Millions."

"That's quite a lot of everything."

"Yes, isn't it, though."

"How's your brother at sharing?"

"He's as stingy as a jaybird. Besides, he hates me. He wouldn't give me the sweat off his brow— that is if he ever had any: He's never done a day's work in his life." She took out a pack of cigarettes from the pocket of her jogging pants. "Cigarette?" she asked.

I took one, then leaned forward and lit hers with the gold table lighter. I appreciated a woman who smoked—there weren't many left. "Then why do you want to spend your money locating your brother if there's nothing in it for you?" I asked.

"Oh, there'll be something in it for me all right."□

"There will? What?"

"His death. If he dies before probate is finished, it all comes to me."

"I see," I said and blew smoke in her direction.

She blew smoke back. "And that's where you come in. I want to share the inheritance with you if you'll find him and kill him."

"I see."

We blew smoke at each other for a while. She finally said, "Interested?"

"A share of a million dollars sounds interesting."

She took a deep puff from her cigarette and quietly tapped a tattoo on the polished rosewood arm of the client's chair while exhaling. "It must take a lot to keep up an office like this," she said, sweeping the hand with the cigarette through the air in front of her.

I looked around at the polished wood furniture, the paneled walls, the Persian carpets, the artwork. I guessed she was right: It must take a lot to keep up an office like this.

"Is that an original Picasso?"

"Only a sketch."

"You have very good taste, Mr. Malory," she said, stamping out her cigarette in my Baccarat ashtray.

"Thank you."

"I love that bouquet of fresh-cut flowers and the crystal vase."□

"Yes."

"Well, will you take my case?"

"I'm afraid you've made me an offer I can't refuse. Yes, I will find your brother and kill him for you."

I heard laughter behind me.

She laughed and said, "I knew you would."

And I knew that she was trouble, but, as she said, it took a lot to keep up an office like this.

The phone rang and she sat stiffly upright. "Don't!" she said.

I looked at her and she looked at me.

I saw the knobs growing on the sides of her head, under the blond hair. Her green eyes burned hot. Her nostrils flared, turning blood red, the fetor of brimstone overpowering her Chanel.

I lurched forward and picked up the phone before it was too late.

My hand clutched the receiver so hard my arm shook. My eyes stared vacantly ahead, peeled wide enough I feared they might become stuck in that position. The thumping of my heart jogged my head.

I heard my name called in the distance by an insect-like voice. I stared at the receiver in my hand, then slowly brought it to my ear.

"Mr. Malory?"

"Yeah," I said, clearing my throat.

"Are you all right, Mr. Malory?"

"Yeah. I'm fine. Who is this?"

"This is Eunice Hammond. I just wanted to check with you to see if you had anything to report yet. I have to go out a lot and sometimes my phone machine doesn't work. I didn't want to miss your call."

I wiped my hand across my face. "As a matter of fact, I may have a line on your brother." I took the receiver from my ear, put my hand over the mouthpiece, then coughed and cleared my throat again. "I should have some hard information for you soon."

"That sounds encouraging. Can you tell me more about it?"

"Not now. I'll get back to you when something develops." I hung up before she could try to wheedle any more out of me.

It was nearly dark out. Rain still pelted the grimy cracked window, the office was its usual dismal self: no carpets, no antique furniture, no Picasso, and no flowers. I hated cut flowers—why bring something inside to die.

It was good to be back home.

The main industry of San Francisco is tourists. People come from all over the country—from all over the world—to see the sights. They come to see the Golden Gate Bridge because the bridge in their little town is just an ugly concrete thing. They come to see Chinatown because they only have two Asian families in their little town. They come to see the cable cars because they only have noisy buses where they're from. But I guess the main thing they don't have back home is breasts because that's where they really line up on Columbus Street, to stand in line to see "the really! really! topless show inside," as the barkers like to say.□

Inside the Orion Club, there was a combo playing: piano, sax, trumpet, and drums. It looked like the piano player was playing in his sleep and the rest were having trouble keeping up.□

On the stage, bathed in a blue light that made her skin look like that of a turkey set out to defrost, was a scrawny topless dancer wearing a G-string and a lot of sequins.

A group of five middle-aged men in front of

the stage was having the time of their lives, calling out war whoops, giving shrill whistles, banging on the table out of time with the music—probably doctors from Des Moines. I moved further into the darkroom.□

There were a couple of empty stools at the bar, but I went to a vacant table. You can usually get better information from a hostess than from a bartender. I sat down, lit a cigarette, and loosened my tie, and waited.□

A cocktail waitress came. She was tall and didn't say anything, just stood over me. "A club soda with two limes," I said.

No smile, no nod, she just turned and headed for the pair of chrome rails at the center of the bar.

She ordered the drink from the bartender, then headed back toward me. She put the glass down and said: "Twenty dollars."

I looked at the small half-full glass, then back up at her. "Twenty dollars? For a half glass of club soda? He didn't even put in any limes."

"First drink's twenty, second's fifteen, then seven-fifty each for the rest. Doesn't matter what you order, all prices the same."

"I see, no cover, no minimum, just gouging drink prices."

She stared at me. I took out my wallet and laid a twenty on the sticky table. Before she could reach for it, I laid another twenty on top of it. "I'd like to buy some information also," I said.

She took the twenty on top and left the other. "I only sell drinks," she said as she walked away.

I took a sip of my twenty-dollar club soda and looked around the room for another open table. I couldn't have any worse luck with a different waitress. But I saw that she was the only one working the floor. At twenty dollars a drink, what could you expect—service too?

Carefully sipping my drink, I waited.

The waitress was waiting on the neurosurgeons from Des Moines. One of them grabbed her from behind and pulled her onto his lap, planting his lips on the back of her neck. I saw her make a quick, sure movement with her elbow to his midsection and he doubled over, dropping his hands from her. She stood up, turned around, and let him have a whack from her tray on the top of his head. He gave a howl I heard above the drone of the band. He stared at her for a moment in disbelief, then reared back his fist, ready to throw a punch. I tensed, wondering how quick I could cross the room. She took her tray again and snapped it edgewise with a lot of wrist action against his forearm. He bellowed. □

Two of his buddies stood up and started moving on her as if they were going to call her out into the alley to fight like a man. I shot my eyes over to the bartender and saw that he was oblivious to the scene.□

I jumped from my chair to go give her a little help, after all, she may have been quicker and smarter, but she was outnumbered.□

The guy she'd let have it with the tray was clutching his arm and moaning. "It's broken! I know it's broken!"

I came between her and the two guys. "Why don't you tough guys just sit back down," I said.

I tried to look real mean and it worked on one of them. The other one was a big guy, almost my size, and he wasn't going to be intimidated that easily.

"She attacked my buddy here," he said to me, fire in his glazed eyes.

"No she didn't," I said. "She defended herself from his gropes."

"I never did anything to her," the guy nursing his sore arm said behind me.

"You hear that?" the big guy said.

I gave him my sternest look. "He was groping her," I said, adding snarl to my voice.

"All he did was give her a kiss on the neck," he snarled back. "What's so wrong about that?"

Even though he was a large guy, I didn't worry about him—he had no finesse. He had come up on me like an umpire comes up to a manager in a dispute. His nose a couple inches from mine, his legs spread wide, his head tilted back. Somehow he'd come to think this was an intimidating posture, probably from coaching Little League. But it was all wrong. His crotch was wide open, his jaw was hanging out in the air just asking for a quick uppercut, and his shoulders were back, totally useless for blocking a swing.

"You know, you're missing the whole point here," I said. "If a girl wants to be kissed on the back of the neck and you kiss her there, that's fine.

If she doesn't and you do, that's assault in my book."

"Yeah?" he said, showing great imagination. I wondered if next he was going to say my mother wore army boots.

He didn't. So, to show that great minds think alike, I said, "Yeah."

"She's a two-bit drink hustler," he said, shortening the distance between our noses by half.

"Suppose I just go behind you and hold your chair like a gentleman so you can sit back down," I said politely. "That would be real nice, don't you think?"

He walked right into it. "And what if I don't want to sit back down," he said.

I threw a short jab to his solar plexus. His cheeks puffed out as he bent in two. He began to sink backward and I hurried behind him to position the chair so that he fell securely into it. I made sure he was breathing all right amidst his gasps and gurgles, then I adjusted his tie and leaned close to his purplish face. "See? Now that's assault."

"Get out," a deep, raspy, voice said.

I turned and saw the bartender holding a black coat out to the waitress. "Go on, I've had it with you. You're out," he said to her.

She grabbed the coat and headed for the door. "Hey wait," I called after her, then turned to the bartender. "You can't do that."

He ignored me and headed back to the bar. The guy with the hurt arm was still whining; the guy I'd had to put down was coughing and swearing; the rest of the group cowered in their seats, wearing their best "I-didn't-say-nothin'" faces. The band played on, the topless dancer listlessly flapping her breasts in the smoky air.

I wondered how I got myself into these kinds of scenes.

I hurried across the room and caught up with the waitress. "I'm sorry," I said.

"It's not your fault," she said.

"No, wait, I'll tell the bartender I started it all."

"Forget it," she said and went out the door.

I followed her outside. "But there's no reason to lose your job. It wasn't your fault."

"I was sick of that dump anyway, so it's okay. Don't worry. It's okay."

She headed up Columbus and I walked alongside. "Maybe I shouldn't have butted in."

"I told you, never mind."

"I don't like seeing people shoved around."

"And I don't like being shoved around."

"Where are you going to go now?"

"None of your business."

"Can I buy you a drink?"

"I don't like bars."

"Okay, how about a cup of coffee?"

We came to a stoplight. She turned to me. "Listen, you don't have to do anything for me. I told you it's okay."

It's funny how people look different in bars. Most women look better in the dim, reddish light. Inside the club, she had seemed worn and hard. Outside, under the light from street lamps and the reflected glare of the passing headlights, she looked different. There was serenity about her, a fundamental dignity. She was tall and dark with dark hair down to her shoulders. Her eyes were Bedouin-dark and very deep.

She looked at me. "You don't have to take care of me. It wasn't your fault. I'm not your responsibility."

"I know," I said.

She smiled. "You know," she mimicked. "I think you're a man who thinks he knows a lot."

I smiled back. "Not a lot. Not a lot at all."

The WALK light came on but I didn't mention it. I was enjoying standing there with her.

"What's your name, tough guy?" she said.

"Frank."

She held out a hand. "I'm Rita."

I took her hand. "Pleased to meet you, Rita."

She stared at me with a strange look for a moment, then said, "You like Italian food, Frank?"

"My last name's Malory," I said with a shrug.

She smiled. "My favorite restaurant's three blocks up."

"Great."

"I'll buy. Reward you for your gallantry."

The WALK light flashed green again and we waited for the stream of speeding cars running the red light, then crossed and headed up Columbus Street.

6

The place was small and crowded with a lot of working people from the clubs and restaurants on Columbus, and there weren't any tourists.

I lit a cigarette and offered her one and she shook her head. "You should quit at your age," she said.

"My age?"

She laughed. "I didn't mean you're old. I meant you should be mature enough to overcome your vices."

I liked the way she laughed, the flash in her dark eyes. A waiter came and she ordered lasagna for both of us. When he had gone, Rita said: "Thank you for what you did."

"I don't like seeing someone pushed around, although it looked like you were handling yourself okay."

"All my life people have felt they could do whatever they wanted to me. I just fight back sometimes."

"Good."

"Sure, good for you. For a man. For a big guy like you. What do you do? Cop?"

"A private detective."

"Do you carry a gun?"

"Sometimes."

"I wish I could carry a gun. It's hard for a woman; there's no place to wear it. I guess I could keep it in my purse." She laughed. "But most of the time when I'd like to shoot somebody, I don't have my purse handy."

"It's not a good idea to go around shooting people."

"A good way to thin out the assholes of the world, as far as I'm concerned."

The food came. It was good lasagna. It only needed a bottle of Chianti to make it perfect. I thought about ordering some but didn't. □

I liked the way she ate, with a sensuous gusto.

"What was that business about information?" she asked. "What were you doing in that tourist dump, anyway?"

"I'm looking for someone."

"Who?"

"A guy by the name of Orin Hammond." Her nose wrinkled and her mouth puckered. "You know him?"

"He hangs out at the club a lot."

"That's what I've been told. Will he be there later tonight?"

"He's away."

"Do you know where?"

"All I care is he's gone."

"What can you tell me about him?"

"He's a two-legged cockroach."

"It sounds like he must have done something awful to you."

"I don't want to talk about it."

"He's in the porno rackets?"

"He's into anything that's rotten. I can't believe anybody'd hire you to find him."

"Just someone's trying to locate him."

"Probably to kill him."

"Nothing like that. Does he have a place on the coast somewhere ?"

"Who told you that?"

"Someone else who doesn't think too highly of him. She's living in his apartment."

"Jill?"

"Kind of short, straight blond hair, young—a girl with a lot of problems."

She finished her lasagna, then said, "That's Jill. She's a naive girl. He made a fool of her."

"She said something about up the coast."

"He's got a cabin out by Dillon Beach."

"Do you know exactly where it is?"

She looked at me with uncertainty, then said, "Yeah, I know where it is."

"Would you tell me how to find it?"

Her face got hard. "What if I don't want to have anything to do with Orin, not even telling a private detective where he might be?"

"I'll find him, anyway. You don't owe me anything."

The waitress came with the check. I reached for

it but Rita snapped it up. "I told you I was taking you to dinner, Sir Gawain," she said.

I took out my wallet. "That's not right." She stared at me like something was wrong. "What's the matter?"

"You're a real old-fashioned guy, aren't you, Frank Malory."

"All right," I said, folding my wallet. "I don't want to be anti-feminist."

"It's not that," she said, still staring at me.

"What then?"

She was silent, then said, "How about if you pay for the drinks."

"Drinks?"

"The ones we are going to order."

I felt a lump form in my throat. "I didn't know we were going to order any."

She turned to the waitress and said, "A big bottle of your finest cheap Chianti, please."

The waitress left and Rita looked at me. "Frank Malory," she said slowly, turning her eyes away. "I'm afraid tonight did me almost in. I am either going to go straight to the Golden Gate Bridge and jump or get very drunk. And I don't want to do either alone."

Her arm rested on the table in front of her, her hand balled into a fist, the skin over her knuckles taut. I laid my hand over hers. "I'll drink to that," I said.

The hand under mine went soft and I wrapped my fingers carefully over it before it could fist up again.

The waitress came with the wine. I still held Rita's hand while I poured, then raised my glass to her. "To Pope Gregory," I proposed.

She smiled and picked up her glass and tapped it against mine.

It was the elixir of the gods, the wine that ran down my throat. Like Odysseus seeing Argos, I had to hide a tear.

Rita refilled our glasses. "After we finish this bottle, I know a place not far from here where we can get a great Irish coffee. I want you to tell me all about yourself, Mr. Frank Malory. About all the damsels you've saved from dragons and all that stuff. Then, at two o'clock, I will stumble to my home and you can stumble to yours and you'll never have to see me again. Okay? Just save my life for tonight. Okay?"

"Sure," I said. "And then you can tell me how to get to that place on the beach."

She smiled. "You don't give up, do you, Mr. Detective Man."

I shrugged.

"Yeah, I'll tell you. I'll draw you a little map." She finished her wine. "You can go out there tomorrow and watch them do their smut on the beach."

I refilled our glasses, then waved to the waitress for another bottle.

7

I was awake yet not awake, dreaming but not dreaming. I floated among clouds, cozy clouds. I smelled smells of balmy flowers. Surrounded by clouds and flowers, I drifted back to sleep.

I awoke languid and relaxed with eyes focused on a ceiling that wasn't the cracked and yellowed ceiling of my office; it was a pretty ceiling, off-white, smooth. I liked this ceiling. I promised I would get myself one to wake up to.

I started to roll onto my side to see what the wall was like and froze halfway over. My eyes darted side-to-side, waiting for the bulldog in my back to bite. He never did. I continued rolling onto my side. Nothing. No pain. I smiled and looked at the wall. The wall was smooth and off-white and fresh, like the ceiling.

There was an antique dresser: dark fruitwood veneer, three drawers, a large tilting center mirror and two side-wing mirrors, scarves in playful pastels draped over one of the side mirrors.

I saw me in the center mirror. I looked younger than I remembered. The pouches under the eyes weren't as puffy, the looseness around the neck wasn't as loose. It was a flattering mirror. Behind my reflection was a long lump in the bed. A willowy olive-skinned arm lay on top of the long lump.

It didn't look like an arm I knew. I closed my eyes and thought: lasagna, Chianti, Irish Coffees, a lot of laughter, nice music in a jazz club, hot brandies in big snifters, flashing dark eyes—then a big blank nothing between the hot brandies in big snifters in a nice jazz club and the mirror with the lump and the long dark-skinned arm.

A name came. Rita—tall, dark-haired, dark-eyed. Young—way too young. We had talked on a street corner.

I rolled over, rejoicing in my loose back. I snaked under the crisp sheets and slid in against her. We were both naked. I wrapped an arm over her and my hand fell against her breast.

She murmured softly, pleasantly. I pulled her tighter against me. She murmured again, deeply, luxuriantly. Good sweaty sex is great, but nothing beats hugging in the morning.□

We stayed that way for a long time, then I started kissing the back of her neck and studying her with my hand.

"Frank?" she said.

"Yes?"

"I mean, is that your name—Frank?"

"Yeah."

"Nice name," she murmured.

"Thanks," I said.

"I don't do this," she said.

"Don't do what?"

"I don't go to bed with men the first time I meet them."

"I should hope not."

She grabbed my hand. "And I don't make love in the morning, either."

"Why not?"

"It's too early. I need to go pee. I haven't brushed my teeth. I just never do it in the morning."

I pulled my hand free and tried to change her mind.

"Frank?" she said, her voice deep.

"Yes?"

"Do you think people change?"

"Certainly."

"Yeah," she said and rolled over hard against me.

Rita had not only drawn me a map to the cabin a few miles above Dillon Beach: but had also loaned me her car to get there—a little rattling, drab gray thing that you had to shift.

As I neared the coast, the sky turned overcast, and soon the sun was lost above high, thick fog. I liked that kind of weather, it made you think the world was a perpetually bright place, that it didn't need a big burning ball traveling the sky for light, that there was no sun to set, that night might never come with its two-legged rats and greedy vipers.☐

I drove past the cluster of houses at Dillon Beach and continued up the coast, watching for the big split cypress that marked the turnoff on Rita's map.

I came to the tree, then followed the rest of the sign points, until I got to a very desolate, windswept stretch, then rattled across a cattle guard and had to navigate slowly through clumps of grazing sheep. Finally, I descended a steep incline and saw the cabin perched on a precipice. There was a Pinkerton Guard van in front of the cabin. I dropped down the rest of the way with the engine off and stopped the car behind a thick tall bush so it couldn't be seen from the cabin. I got out and headed for the edge of the cliff that led down to the ocean.☐

It was a sheer drop of a couple hundred feet, and I could see why they had chosen this place: There was a small beach of smooth sand enclosed by rocky cliffs that jutted out into the ocean on both sides with the only access from the cabin a narrow path that snaked across the face of the cliff. The guard was probably stationed at the cabin.

I lowered myself to a shelf that ran across the face of the cliff and was able to inch my way to the path without coming into view from the cabin.

Carefully climbing down, I saw some people gathered in the center of the beach. They were very intent on what they were doing and paid no attention to the cliff side. With luck, I would be able to climb all the way down unnoticed.☐

I dropped onto the beach and made my way to where they were working. When I got near, I knew it had to be him. He was seated in a tattered, orange canvas-backed director's chair, his lips wrapped around a cigar, a thick gold chain circling his neck, a heavy gold bracelet in the shape of a bicycle chain on his wrist, a large gold and onyx ring with a diamond on the fat finger of his pudgy left hand.

Next to him was a woman with a clipboard. In front of them was a cameraman with a professional video camera and a soundman with a boom that he held out over the heads of the two on the sand.

The two on the sand, around whom all attention was focused, were a naked woman under a naked man who was thrusting away on her like a rutting bull. I had watched X-rated movies on occasion, but it was different seeing one in the flesh.

I walked up next to the man in the orange director's chair. "Mr. Orin Hammond?"

He looked at me in startled disbelief, as if I had materialized out of the air. "What's this?" he finally said. "What the fuck's this?"

"My name is Frank Malory," I told him.

"I don't give a shit if your name is Grandpa Moses! Get the fuck off my beach. This is a private beach! How the fuck did you get down here, anyway?" He turned to his assistant. "Mary, get Jake on the walkie-talkie and ask him who the hell this is and what's he doing here."

"I've been hired to locate you, Mr. Hammond,"

I said.

"Listen, you don't talk. You're not here. No one is allowed here. This is a private place, got it? So don't talk. You're not here!"

"Civil code section 309, paragraph 41, subsection b, 'No part of the California coastline may be deemed as private property,'" I concocted on the spot.□

All this time the cigar had hung from his lips, bouncing up and down, shaking ash over the front of him. He stared at me and slowly removed the cigar. "You from the DA's office? You here to bust us? 'Cause if you are, you can't. We're in our legal rights here."

"I'm not here to bust you," I told him.

He pointed his cigar at me. "Don't talk, don't even talk. I told you, you're not here!"

He pitched out of his chair. "Mary, godammit, I told you I want Jake on the goddamn walky-talky."

She looked down at the sand. "We don't have the walky-talkies, Mr. Hammond. Remember, the batteries are dead."

"Shit!" he said and threw his cigar to the sand. "Shit!"

He turned back to me. "How'd you get here, fella? Do you know there's a guy up there with a gun? A guy who's hired to shoot people who try to trespass. A Pinkerton guard with a gun."

"I'm a private detective and I've been hired to locate you by someone who wants to talk with you."

"Go fuck yourself, Jack," he suggested, then turned and headed for the path to the cabin. "I'm going up and get Jake and his gun and you're history around here, fella. I don't know what your game is. But however you got here, you better get the hell back outa here the same way."

He started up the path. I turned to see what the rest of the crew was doing: The cameraman and sound technician were sitting on a rock smoking, Mary just stood with a look of worried confusion on her face, the naked man was sprawled on the sand snoring. The naked woman approached me. "You don't seem like you're too worried about Orin and his gun-toting honcho," she said.

"I worry about guys with guns," I told her. "But I'm here on a case."

"Got a cigarette?" she said. "I don't have my purse on me at the moment." I tapped one from the pack and held it out to her, then took one for myself and gave her a light. "You come here to bust us?" she said, exhaling smoke.

"No."

It was strange standing on the beach, having a conversation with a naked woman. She was short and small-boned, her skin a sensitive pinkish tone, her body tight and in good shape. I guessed her to be in her mid-twenties. Somehow, it didn't seem that unnatural for her to be naked. "Would you be able to tell me where Orin is currently staying?" I asked.

"Sure," she said to my surprise. "He'll probably be at the cabin tonight and then, starting tomorrow, if we wrap things up here, he'll be staying at my place for two weeks while I go back to visit my parents in South Dakota." She laughed. "He's been tossed out of his place by a girl with a gun."

Sometimes you only have to ask. "And could you give me your address?"

"Why not. It's eleven-twenty-three Bancroft, Room D, in Berkeley. I'm finishing my last year of graduate work at U.C. This is how I support myself until I get my master's in clinical psychology. Guess what my thesis is."□

"What?"

"The Psychopathology of Pornography. In a sense, I'm doing my research here. Orin's my little rat in a maze—he's very pathological."

"Nobody seems to like him much."

"He's quite a ratty person."

I looked up and saw Orin and a uniformed guard starting down the path. "Is there any other way out of here?" I said.

"Nope. The only way in or out is up the cliff."

"Well, I'll just wait for the escort, then."

We smoked our cigarettes and watched the two struggle down the path. "Did you ever figure out your rat?" I asked. "What makes him so nasty?"

"You know, I hate to admit it, but I think it comes down to something as simple as some men are just born sociopath, born incapable of doing anything good."

"I know what you mean," I said.

Orin and his hired gun made it down to the

beach, huffing and puffing as they approached us. "All right, fella, let's be movin' along," the guard said. He was an old guy, probably retired cop. He had short gnarled red hair and reddish freckles. He put a hand on my shoulder and squeezed. "Off we go, buster."

"Take your hand off," I told him calmly.

He only squeezed harder. "I'm giving you a chance to come along peaceably now."

I spun my arm, breaking his grip, giving his arm an extra twirl to slam it against his side. He yelped like a pup wrapped on the nose. "You bastard," he said, and went for the gun in the weathered holster at his side.

I waited till the weapon cleared the holster, then gave him a solid chop to the forearm, not enough to break bone, but enough to splay the short fat fingers, sending his gun to the sand.

He staggered back a step.

Orin moved for the gun. I pulled the Colt from its shoulder holster under my coat and pointed it at Orin. 'Let it lie there," I told him.

I picked up the pistol and slipped it into my coat pocket, then turned to the guard who was bent at the waist clutching his arm. "I'll drop your piece off at the cabin."

If he'd had a tail, it would have been wrapped tightly between his legs. Orin was another matter, if he could kill with just his eyes, I'd be dead. His little kingdom had been violated and he wasn't happy about it. There would be hell to pay when I was gone. I kept my eye on him as I backed to the cliff.

On the climb up I made sure no one followed. When I got to the top I went inside the cabin. There was a high-ceilinged main room whose floor looked like a forest of camera and light tripods. A long table held Moviolas and sound recording equipment. Off the main room was a bedroom almost filled by a round bed with an orange fake fur spread. The ceiling was fully mirrored and one complete wall was all mirror of that unusual vacant cast that I was familiar with: a one-way mirror.

I pulled out the Colt and slammed the butt into the center of the wall mirror. The glass cracked, then collapsed into large shards and there it was. I carefully aimed at the center of the gaping lens and fired.

I tossed the guard's revolver onto the bed and went out to the car.

On the drive back to San Francisco, I was a man pleased with himself. It had been a worthwhile case and I'd handled it okay. I'd proved that I didn't have a drinking problem. That was news worth celebrating. I decided I'd take Rita out for dinner and dancing somewhere other than The Strip. Maybe the Mark Hopkins—I still had some of the retainer left.

When I got back to Rita's there was a note taped next to the doorbell. It said she had to fly to L.A. because of an illness in the family, and could I slide the car key under the door, and she'd maybe call me when she got back. I slid the key under the door, tore the note off, crumpled it, and shoved it into my pocket.

Sitting at the bus stop on the corner, I played catch with the crumpled note. The sky was sun-washed clear blue, the sun bright and almost warm: a good day for finishing up some business and maybe taking a walk around Stow Lake before getting cleaned up to go out with an interesting woman you've just met; the kind of things a young man does. I'd had my days in the sun, my walks in the park, my nights at the Top of the Mark. I tossed the balled-up note into the trash barrel at the end of the bench. No regrets.

The bus came, I climbed aboard.

Back at my office, I picked up the mail off the floor where it had tumbled from the slot in the door, then I dropped into my chair to see what the world at large had sent me. Amnesty International said they could use another donation and included a free bumper sticker. Too bad I didn't have a bumper to stick it on right at the moment. There was a forwarded PG&E bill threatening to turn off the power to the apartment I had been evicted from three months ago. "Freedom's just another word for nothin' left to lose," I hummed and sailed the bill into the dented wastebasket. Ed McMahon smiled up at me from his golden brown envelope and told me I, too, could win fifteen million dollars if I acted real fast. I sent Ed down to discuss the matter with PG&E. A guy named Crazy Freddie looked out at me from a four-color flyer, his eyes crossed, his tie on sideways and his tongue dangling the side of his mouth. He told me he was forced to sell color TVs under his cost because his warehouse manager had over-ordered. His loss was my gain. Maybe Ed could use a new set. The rest was too uninteresting to even bother opening.□

Anyway, I'd finished a case in record time. I was back in business again. I pulled out the file for her number, then picked up the phone and dialed. I got her answering machine, and I left the information where Orin could be found. Job finished, retainer fully earned.

8

I was dreaming about the crow and the skull with dried-up brains again. His pecking was sharper now. Then I woke up. It was tapping at the pebble glass of my door I was hearing. I had fallen asleep at my desk again, the office was turning into an old folks home for one. For some reason I grabbed my gun out of the shoulder holster I was still wearing. The lighted clock on my desk showed a little after midnight. They must have been late in locking the street door. A caller at this hour had to mean trouble.

I went cautiously to the door. The dim bulb in the hallway showed a silhouette against the opaque glass of someone slight. So what, they came in all sizes. I chambered a shell and slipped off the safety. Intuition.

"Frank?" she said. "Are you in there?"

I carefully let the hammer down and turned the safety. "Rita?" I said.

"Can you let me in, Frank?"

I opened the door. She stood there in the

yellow light dressed in jeans and a man's white dress shirt. She had on slippers. I said, "What's wrong?"

"Can I come in?"

I stood back from the door.

I shut the door and started for the desk chair. "Not there," she said.

I looked at her.

"The couch."

I nodded. We went to the couch. "I haven't slept," she said, sitting down close to me.

"It's not that late," I said.

"No. I mean I haven't hardly slept since I met you."

"Yeah? . . ." I said.

She looked disheveled, her hair twisted, her eyes a little deep-set, no makeup—she was beautiful. "Go on," I said.☐

"I'm afraid," she said, her voice soft.

"Of what?"

"Of you. Me."

"Tell me. . . ."

"I didn't go to L.A.," she said. "I don't have any family there, sick or otherwise."

Suddenly I was afraid too. "You just made that up."☐

"That's right. No, I didn't just make it up—I lied. I have got to start facing myself. Stop running. I lied to you, Frank."

"I understand."

"I heard your footsteps come up the hall. I saw the key come under the door. I stood there and saw it slide through. And I cried. I wanted to throw the door open and run after you. Like in some silly movie."

I put my arm around her. She tipped into me and I could feel the ripple of release that ran through her. She said, so softly I could barely hear, "I never knew my father. He died before I was born. Understand? A father was what other kids had. You know what I mean? I used to watch them, the other kids' fathers when I'd go to their house. I'd wonder—is that the way he would have walked? Would he have talked like that? Their fathers taught them things, you know. How to ride a bike. Roller skate. Father things. You see what I mean?"

I held her a little tighter. "Yeah."

"What I'm trying to say is that it's like an empty space."

She pulled away from me enough to look into my face. The moonlight through the blinds painted stripes on her face. "You don't know what I'm saying do you, Frank?"

"I do."

"Do I sound crazy?"

"No."

"I keep falling in love with men older than me. Don't laugh, but I even go to this group. Yeah, they've got a group for it. They tell us it's like a sickness. Like the way a person drinks too much or takes drugs. That we're trying to run away from facing something. They try to make us go out with men our own age."

She curled back tight against me. "But I can't do it with them. I can't get any feeling. I don't care if I'm sick like they say. I've got to have feeling or I'm dead. You understand?"

"I do."

"Everybody's got to have feeling, don't they, Frank? No matter why they have them?"

"Sure," I said.

"I think not having feeling is what is sick."

"I think you're right."

"Can I stay here tonight, Frank?"

"Yes."

"Can we lay down on this couch and you just hold me. Just for tonight if you want. Not make love or anything. Just hold me. So I can at least sleep for tonight."

"Yes," I said, the fear wafting through me.

I woke up with Rita wrapped tightly around me and the phone ringing. Outside the window, it was grim daylight. I decided to answer and carefully slipped myself free of Rita who still lay soundly curled.

"Mr. Malory?" Her voice was tight and twisted as if someone was holding a gun to her head.

"Eunice?" I said.

"He— He—" Then silence.

"Eunice? You still there?"

More silence. Then, "He tried to hurt me, Mr. Malory. My own brother. My own brother tried to hurt me."

"What happened? Where are you?"

"I'm over near that dingy place where you told

me I could find him. It was terribly messy."

"Is he there with you?"

"No. I ran off when he got so awful. I'm at a payphone on a noisy street in front of some store that sells liquor and cigarettes."☐

"Have you got a car? Get out of there."

"I came by bus."

"Then hop the next bus that comes by."

"But I think it's all just a misunderstanding. I believe he got upset that I hired you to find him. Maybe if you came over and explained things he will understand."

"Listen to me. Your brother is a dangerous man. You've got to get away from him right now. Hang up and dial 911 for the police. Have them send a car for you."

"Oh, I couldn't involve the police regarding my own brother. They might arrest him or something."☐

"Can you see the name of the liquor store?"

Silence, then, "It says The White Horse or The White House, I can't tell for sure. The painting is all old and chipped."☐

"The White Horse," I said, "I know it. You're just a few blocks from him. Now stay there. Just stay in the phone booth or stand by the door of the liquor store. If he comes after you, run inside and tell the clerk to call the police. Got that."

"All right. You're going to come over, then? And talk to him?"

"Just wait right there."

I wasn't going to have another dead client on my hands.

I woke up Rita, who first looked at me like I was some stranger, then said my name and smiled. I told her I had an emergency with a client in Berkeley and she immediately scrambled for her purse on the floor and got out the car keys. "I'll take care of myself," she said.

She wasn't there—not at the phone booth and not in front of the liquor store. I went inside and looked around. I went to the old guy on a stool behind the counter and asked if a woman had been in for help, and he looked at me with thick-lidded, weary eyes as he shook his head.

I got back into Rita's car and drove the two blocks to Bancroft. I found 1123, the room the naked woman on the beach had loaned out to Orin. It was a typical U.C. student neighborhood of worn down, sad houses.

A black Mercedes with darkened windows and a car phone antenna started up half a block away. Wealthy parents visiting.

I made my way through the bags of beer cans and tried the handle of the front door. As with most rooming houses in a college neighborhood, it was unlocked.

The door marked D was at the end of a hall with walls of cracked plaster and flaking hospital-green paint. I listened for arguing voices. There weren't any. I put my ear against the door—still nothing. I tried the handle. This one, too, was unlocked.

I stuck my head cautiously inside. I looked

around. It was what you would expect of a graduate student's room—bookshelf of cinder block and yellowed cheap pine boards, a Pullman kitchen in the corner with dishes and coffee cups and pots stacked precariously, a small spindly-legged table painted Chinese red.

"Anyone?" I called out. No answer. "Hello?" Still nothing. There was no bed and not enough room on any wall for a wall bed. The door to the left of the couch must lead to a bedroom. Orin might be asleep there.

Remembering the murderous look he'd given me on our last encounter, I took out the Colt, chambered a round, and released the safety. I held the pistol muzzle up while I tiptoed to the door. I gingerly swung the door open and looked inside.□

He *was* on the bed. I let the Colt slowly hang to my side. I was the second one to arrive with a gun.

His eyes were open and so was his mouth. A lot of blood had run out his mouth, forming a black sticky pool around his head, like a satanic halo. The look on his wide eyes was one of shocked surprise.

A fly buzzed, then landed on the corner of his mouth. It scampered inside, found what it was looking for, and came flying out.□

I hated being the first one on a shooting scene. Something like the business with the fly always happened, something that would pop into my consciousness later, usually while I was trying to get to sleep.

All I could register was that this made no sense.

Where was his sister? Who the hell had shot him? Why? Was it a double murder? Was her body somewhere around?

I pulled out the gun again and carefully approached the open door of the bathroom. No one. There was a shower but the curtain was pulled back. No one there either.

I forced myself to examine the body. There were several small caliber holes through the thin cloth of his white double-knit shirt, a ragged cluster of hits across his large abdomen. The gun was fired at close range, there were powder burns on his shirt and they had that tight smoke ring look that indicated a silencer. A professional? Yet the spread of the shots spoke of a killer who was a bad marksman.

I rolled his body over a little. There were no exit wounds. That would point to the reduced muzzle velocity of a small-caliber handgun with silencer. Probably a revolver because there were no shell casings around.☐

I let him roll back, then pulled his coat up and tugged the shirt out from the pants and touched the skin of his stomach, then reached below him and did the same thing to his back. He hadn't been dead long. I lifted his arm and it bent freely at the elbow. I let the arm fall to the bed—hours, no longer, probably less.

The fly returned, landing on the lip. I waved it away.

I saw the bulge of a wallet still in his hip pocket; his full complement of gold still encircled neck and wrist. It hadn't been a local junkie he'd surprised in the act. And they don't run around with silencers anyway. Someone had just plain wanted him dead. From what I'd learned of him so far, that left a long list of suspects.

"Drop the gun! NOW!"

It all flashed through my mind as quickly as a bullet. If the voice behind me was the killer there wouldn't have been any orders, I'd just be lying dead next to Orin. That "NOW!" spoke of a cop. At least I had a chance. "Hammer's back and I don't trust this old thing to drop it on the hard floor. Don't want a misfire. I'm going to toss it onto the bed to be safe."

"Drop the gun! NOW!"

I gave the pistol a careful toss onto the bed.

"Hands behind your back!"

I did as he said. "Not so tight," I told him after he'd snapped the cuffs on.

"Walk," was all he said. "Out to the patrol car in front."

I slept the next two nights on a steel cot in the Berkeley city jail holding cell, swapping stories of the good old days with fellow detainees who were old enough to remember them and others who were young enough to find them interesting. My only concern was that I might cross paths with some bounty-jumper I'd drug back years ago, but that didn't happen. I figured that most of them had died in jail or gotten old enough to finally go straight.□

On the third day, a starchy outfitted duty cop came and told me I was to meet with the detective handling the case. I got up and straightened out my orange jumpsuit and followed him to the changing room where I got back into my civilian clothes.

We went past the filthy lock-ups and drunk tanks and down the dim and dirty hallway past the interrogation rooms until we came to a flight of carpeted stairs leading to the administration offices, then on through a wide room of detectives drinking coffee and smoking as they slowly two-finger typed out their reports on high-speed computers, finally coming to a heavy oaken door with a brass plaque announcing, RICHARD HOMES CHIEF OF DETECTIVES. The cop knocked and waited. Then, "Bring him in," came from behind the door.

I followed the cop into the room, and he pointed to the single chair facing the large polished desk. I took the chair and the cop left. I waited while Chief of Detectives Richard Homes ignored me, chatting and laughing a few minutes more, then telling the phone he had to tend to some business. It was probably an empty line.

He made notes on a yellow legal pad, then looked up at me as if suddenly realizing I was there. "You look like hell, Frank," he said.

"Haven't been sleeping well," I told him.

He rocked back in his leather judge's chair and stared at me. "I don't like it when a cop goes bad," he said as if I represented some type of contagion to him.

"Neither do I," I said.

"You were a good detective back in San Francisco when you helped me through the ranks."

"The good old days," I said.

"Yes. The good old days." He gave me a penetrating stare. "I have been following your career, my old friend. You have been on a downhill path ever since you quit the force."

Richard Homes was a company man, a Disraeli to the upper echelons of movers and shakers, someone who took care of what needed taking care of so those above him could look clean and wholesome. I had disliked him from his early days as a detective when he'd come to me for help after stepping on too many toes in his over-eagerness to succeed.□

"Am I to be released?" I said.

He looked at me over the top of his gold-rimmed reading glasses. "You killed that scum bag. I know it and you know it."

"What does the DA's office have to say about it."

His eyes narrowed. "Fuck the DA's office."

"I guess I'm to be released, then."

He took a cigarette from the pack on his desk without offering me one. "Here is the way I see it, Frank," he began with an exhale of smoke. "You had a tough cut from the deck, all right, we all do one time or another. But a lot of guys have their wife knocked out from under them and they go on."

I stood up. "Am I still under arrest or not."

"Sit down, Frank. Sit down. You don't get out until I sign the paperwork from the DA's office. I might lose my pen for the rest of the day."

I sat down. He went on. "Frank—you got your pins knocked out from under you and you left the force in San Francisco. You drifted around. All right, who can really blame you? But then you went bad. Look at you. You look like you were just cranked out of a sausage machine."□

I sat and listened because I had to.

He went on: "So, you have probably been working as an enforcer for who knows what organizations—hired muscle but getting too old for it. So now you have turned hitman. And I am going to have to put you away for it."□

I leaned forward and took one of the matching gold-filled pens from the holder on his desk and held it toward him. He reared a hand back to slap my hand away, then must have realized it would break up the set if the pen got broken.

"You've got the whole thing worked out as two weeks of front-page coverage in the Tribune of your campaign against police corruption, don't you."□

He gave me what was supposed to be a menacing stare. I said, "Sign the damn release, Dick."

He pushed a button on his desk and I heard the buzzer go off outside the door. The starched cop who had escorted me came back in.

"Don't go too far away; Frank, I will be reeling you back in soon." He turned to the officer. "Get him out of here," he said as he scribbled his signature on the papers before him.

At the door, I turned back. "I want to have a look at the evidence folder on my case." □

He looked up at me with a slow smile and calmly shook his head.

"I was set up and I think I know by who."

"Tell it to the judge," he said.

I took a bus to Bancroft. Rita's car was still there, street sweeping towing wasn't for another day. I drove back to San Francisco and my office.

The door was wide open and something was making a loud noise inside. I stood cautiously in the doorway. Rita, her back to me, was bent over a vacuum. I knocked on the doorjamb but she didn't hear me. I went to the desk and sat in my chair that was slippery with wood polish. She was humming some innocuous show tune I couldn't quite place.

She shut off the vacuum and turned and saw me in the chair. She yelped.

"I knocked," I said.

"Why didn't you call?"

"I didn't know you'd still be here. I thought I'd call you at home when I got back to my office."

She pulled the bandana off her head and flung her dark hair free. She came and leaned against the edge of the desk. "Have you been away on a case? You don't look good," she said.

"Thanks."

"No, I mean, you look like you've had a rough time."

"I did. I spent the last two nights in the Berkeley jail and I'm getting too old for this kind of shit."

"You got arrested?"

"Yeah."

"Why?"

"For murder."

"Seriously?"

"Very."

"You didn't kill Orin, did you?"

"No. But somebody else did and set me up for it."

"Is everything going to be all right?"

"Yeah," I said as I looked around the office: the crusty sink was somehow polished back to white enamel; the cracked mirror was replaced with a beveled one in a thick black frame; the green file cabinet looked a different shade without its years of grime; the softwood floor had been polished, and there was a small Oriental rug between the door and the desk that triggered the remembrance of a dream.□

"Don't be upset, Frank," she said with a sigh. "Just indulge me. I don't have a job now and I needed to feel some self-worth."□

I nodded.

"I know I have no right to come in and invade your territory just because we fucked once."

I smiled. What else could you do when a woman has been that honest with you. I grabbed her arm and pulled her onto my lap and kissed her—too long and too deeply, I didn't need more complexity in my life right then.

I looked over at the couch; there was a new pillow and blanket on it. "Have you been here the whole time?"

"Timmy can take care of himself."

"You have a child?"

"A cat."

"Oh."

She got up. "Although I'd better get home and check on him."

She grabbed up the car keys I had laid on the desk and was out the door, closing it gently behind her before I could think of anything to say.

I went to the bottom drawer of the now shiny green file cabinet and looked for a bottle. There wasn't one, because I had been proving to myself that I didn't need to drink. Well, maybe I'd proven enough for now, and maybe not drinking had been what had landed me in jail. No, that was stupid. I was just thirsty—thirsty for relief from myself.

I got the key from out of the desk and opened the top file cabinet drawer, where I kept case records. Reaching way into the back, my straining fingers were able to wrap around the comforting feel of a bottle's neck.

Back at my desk, I forced myself to wait long enough to pull the pony glass out of the bottom desk drawer.☐

It's funny the way the first drink makes you feel. Before, the world seems all askew, a spinning, indecisive mass of meaninglessness that covers you like hot road tar just waiting for the spray of feathers. Then, the drink, and instantly you begin to wonder what the trouble had all been about. You feel like you fall into yourself, suddenly become a focus, the split images coalescing into a calm whole. You're back from your slipped moorings.

I pulled the damn Colt from its shoulder holster and dropped it onto the desk with a thud; it had started feeling like some kind of growth. The image came back to me of that fly entering poor dead Orin's mouth ready to start the process of redistributing his atoms to lesser and greater beings. Orin had been a bad guy, but he was one of us, a part of the human family, and he hadn't deserved to be yanked down to hell prematurely.

I stared down at the Colt laid out like a corpse. I had gotten so used to lugging the thing around, I'd forgotten its true intention: a device for tearing holes through human flesh, ripping apart internal organs, shattering bone—for stealing the lives out of people—a loathsome thing to do, even when necessary.

I finished my drink, then picked up the Colt and dropped the magazine from its butt, and thumbed out a round.☐

Looked at it in all its nakedness, it was really only the old rock, like the one David put in his sling—same rock, fancier slingshot. And someone had thrown a handful of those rocks against Orin's body. For some reason. And that someone had called me so I would be set up for a patsy. That sequence of events: the phone call, the disappearance, the cop showing up just in time was no coincidence.

And then the image of the fly faded to be replaced with the dark Mercedes pulling away as I approached the rooming house. I searched the image and there it was: a car phone antenna sticking up above the center of the rear window.

I poured another drink to clear my mind. But it didn't make any sense. It was all a rumble of confusion. Who was the sister? What was her connection with her brother? Was Orin really her brother? Brother or not, why did she want him dead?

I still held the cartridge between thumb and forefinger, and dropped it to the desk. It hit with a determined metallic thunk, then rolled back and forth like the swing of a pendulum—biding its time.

I filled the pony glass and took it with me to the couch. When my head collapsed on her pillow, a waft of her aroma came out. What was I doing here alone? Who killed Orin?

Who was Eunice? What was I doing here alone?

Waking in pain and darkness, I stumbled toward the light switch across the room.

No light.

"Give me some light before I go mad!"

I knew I was yelling to no one but couldn't stop.

I slammed back against the wall.

Like a man lost in the snow, I was dying inch by inch, the cold eating me from the extremities inward.

If I'd had my gun, I might have put it to my temple.

I hate darkness. I fear it. In the darkness, there was only me, and I couldn't stand the sight of myself.□

Was there comfort in the cold of the muzzle against your head?

Do you hear the shot? Feel the slug enter your brain? Cold or hot?

Like the single apple that wouldn't fall from the tree, I hung rotting in winter.

The phone rang—a beacon in the darkness. I grabbed for it. "That you there, Frank?" Eddy's voice said.

Rubbing my hand across my face, I tried to talk.

"You there, Frank?" he said.

"Yeah," I finally got out.

"You okay, Frank?"

"Yeah," I said.

"Say listen, Frank, it's none a my business but she's been comin' down here every night since you was last in."

"Who? "

"Sam," he said. "She's down here now, sittin' at your old table. I don't think she's doin' too good. Maybe you should come on down?"

"Don't let her leave, I'll be right there," I said and hung up.

I bumped my way through the office, aiming for the dim yellow light on the other side of the pebbled glass of the door, then limped to the bathroom at the end of the hall and cleaned myself up as best I could, then hurried down to Eddy's.
There were three or four customers at the bar and a few more at the tables. She sat with her back to me, looking up at the trio playing on the tiny stage. I nodded to Eddy, who nodded back from behind the bar.

I sat down and she continued watching the trio. She didn't look good—eyes puffy, face drawn. "What's new?" I said.

"Nice trio," she said calmly.

We sat in silence. Eddy brought us a bottle of Scotch and glasses and left without saying anything.

"Why do they do it, Frank?" Sam said after a while.☐

"Who does what?" I said.

"Why do women go through the whole goddamn routine of marrying a man they don't love?"

"They must think it's a good idea at the time."

"It's like a death wish."

"We all make mistakes."

"Frank, godammit, I'm forty-two years old—when am I ever going to learn my lesson?"

"People get stuck in patterns."

She looked at me, eyes probing as if I was suddenly a stranger sitting across the table from her. "How come *we* never got married, Frank?"

"The young debutante and the old drunk?"

"Things were good for us once. What happened?"

"My life went sour."

"You were adjusted to losing your wife when we met. Then that terrible woman who got killed. It wasn't your fault."

"She was my client. My responsibility."

"The woman was a criminal. She lied to you."

I took another drink and refilled my glass. "She was my client."

"You make me so goddamn angry, Frank."

"Sorry."

Even in the dim light, I could see that her face was reddening. "Dammit, Frank, don't say that. We were good together. Everything was good. Then you got involved with that woman, and when she got killed, you became a drunk again. You closed up. You took off and left me standing naked in the wind."

"I blew the case."

"We could have gone through it together. You didn't have to throw away everything we had."

"What can I say now?"

"You could say you want to make love to me. You could say you can't stand being without me."

I didn't say anything. She took the bottle, poured, and gulped. "I'm in a bad place right now, Frank. If you have to, lie to me. Just say something good."

"What's happened with you and Terry?"

She tilted her empty glass and looked into it. "He's thrown me out on my ass," she said.

I looked at her carefully in the dim light, there was puffiness to the left side of her face. "He hit you?"

She refilled her glass and took a drink. "What if he did? Are you going to go over with your gun and shoot him?"

"Maybe," I said.

"You probably would, you old fool."

I leaned across the table and she turned the left side of her face away from me. "He did hit you."

She looked down. "Not any harder than I deserved."

"What are you talking about?"

She looked up at me, her eyes somber. "I was coming at him with a fireplace poker."

"You're not going back tonight, are you?"

"I'll go to a hotel."

"I don't want you going back to him tonight."

She stared at me stonily. "You never answered my question."

"What question?"

"You know what question. Why don't you want me anymore?"

"You're a married woman."

"Not for much longer. You've found someone else, haven't you?"

I didn't say anything.

She said, "It's funny, you know. It really is, but I could tell when it was happening. I just felt something in a little corner inside. Do you think things like that travel through the air? Like TV programs? That we have little antennae somewhere inside us picking them up?"

"It's not somebody else. I've just crashed another case."

"What happened?"

"The subject of a case I was working on ended up shot to death."

She looked at me with chastising eyes. "Why do you hang around in that rotten world of yours?"

"That's a question I've been asking more and more lately."

"You've got a lot of talent and brains, Frank. You could have been an attorney." She laughed and fell back into her chair. "Another trap women fall into. They always want to change men. For God's sake, I married a fucking attorney and just got through trying to smash his brains out with a poker. No, you're right, you're a lot better off than if you'd been an attorney."

The trio started playing "Summertime." She got up and grabbed my hand. I followed her to the dance floor. She felt good in my arms like we'd gone back right to where we'd left off, even if we couldn't.

We moved with the slow beat of the music, and she hummed the lyrics softly.

The song ended way too soon. She whispered hoarsely into my ear: *"There ain't nothin' can harm you with your daddy and mammy standin' by* . . . Be with me tonight. Just tonight, Frank. That's all I'll ask. I don't want to be alone right now."

We walked hand in hand past the table. I grabbed the bottle of Scotch, and we smiled goodbye to Eddy as we passed the bar. The ends of his smile didn't quite stretch to his ears.

We slept snuggled together on the couch in my office, both our heads on Rita's pillow, her blanket over us against the cold. My world always seems to land in strange places.

When the sun started lighting the window, Sam got up and kissed me gently on the lips. I pretended sleep and let her slip out of the office. She had things she needed to work out on her own and so did I.

After she was gone, I went downstairs to the landlord's office and settled the electric bill, then brought the receipt to Horace, the maintenance man, who was powering up the boilers. He went to the wall and threw the switch to turn my electricity back on.

9

"This is Eunice. I'm not able to come to the phone right now. Please leave your message at the sound of the tone."

It was the tenth time I'd heard the message in as many minutes. I hung up again.

She was either real good at controlling her curiosity or really not there.☐

I rummaged through the middle desk drawer for my list of phone numbers no one is supposed to have and looked up the telephone company's C.N.A. number for L.A.☐

"This is Jonathan with MCI accounting, up in Gualala," I said in an assured nasal voice when someone answered.

"Hello, Jonathan, how're the salmon running?"

"Not bad. I was driving slow over the bridge yesterday and two of them jumped into my back seat." He laughed. "Hey, listen we've got a problem up here with a third party bill-back on an unlisted. The destination party's in your area and has a P.O. box number for a billing address. We have to serve a small claims warrant and need a physical location. Think you could check with your installation file for the address? Number is two-one-three, five-nine-seven, six-two-five-nine."

I heard tapping at the keys of a terminal. "That's a new install. Hookup was only ten days ago. Address is nine-twenty-seven Florence Street, North Hollywood, apartment seven-twenty. Single box in the living room. Service in the name of a Eunice Hammond."

"Thanks," I said and hung up.

I took a taxi to the airport and left on the next hourly flight to L.A.□

Florence Street wasn't a posh section of town, but there were not too many people living out of shopping carts, either. The apartment building was ten stories and took up half a block. I rode the elevator to the seventh floor and went down the hall to room seven-twenty.

There was no answer to my knock. It was an older building and the door handle looked easy, but there was a retrofitted Schlage deadbolt that looked tough. Just in case, I tried the handle. To my surprise, it turned and the door opened.

No one was home. No one had ever been home—the place was empty.

It was a studio, one large room with a bow window covered by heavy green drapes drawn tight. In the corner, sitting on the dusty hardwood floor, was an answering machine.

I squatted and pushed the announcement

button. "This is Eunice. I'm not able to come to the phone right now. Please leave your message at the sound of the tone."

The shrill beep resonated through the hollow apartment.

I went down to the mailboxes and found the number for the manager's apartment.

I rang the doorbell and stood back. A short, hefty woman in her late sixties, wearing a worn pink chenille bathrobe and curlers, with the face of an attractive bulldog, opened the door. "Yeah?" she said, giving me a quick look up and down.

I took out the phony FBI I.D. I always carry in my wallet. "Agent Malory," I said.

She looked at the card, then back at me. "So?"

"You recently rented room seven-twenty to a single woman. We need to know any information you have about her."

She squinted at me, then said, "Why?"

"Just a routine background check," I said.

She gave me another look, then tightened the sash of her chenille robe and backed into the apartment. "Come on in; I'll check my records."

I doubted the Vatican had more religious artifacts; there must have been fifty or more plastic dashboard St. Christophers stacked around the room. There were crucifixes ranging from a life-size translucent one illuminated from within to necklace-sized silver ones spilling out of cigar boxes.

"You must be a very religious person," I said.

"Me? Hell no. I work part-time down at the St.

Vincent. I skim this crap off what comes in; take it home here and sell it mail order. Supplement's my pension. Though, since that Jimmy and Tammy fiasco, business has fallen way off. This crap is backing up around my ears. I shoulda stayed with dolls. They got more staying power."

She drew a stained and crumpled file folder out of a cardboard box and motioned with her head for me to follow her into the kitchen.

She slapped the file folder on the chrome and yellow Formica dinette and told me to sit down, then took two export bottles of Budweiser out of a case atop the refrigerator and came back to the table and set one of the beers in front of me. "I like it warm. I hear in England everybody drinks it that way." She opened hers and slid the opener across to me. "Be careful, it can spray."□

I opened my beer carefully. "Can I see the file," I said?" handing her back the opener.

She looked at me, then sat down across the table and said: "You ain't FBI." She took a healthy swig from her beer while she kept staring at me. "Hair's too long and the eyes aren't right, they look like they got some brains behind 'em." She took another pull on her beer and belched. "You're not LAPD, either. 'Cause if you was you wouldn't have to throw that line of bull about being FBI." She laughed and killed the bottle of beer. She stood up and got another one. "My old man's been twenty-five years LAPD," she said. "So don't think you're going to pull any crap on me." She sat down and carefully pried the cap off the bottle. I was a little surprised she hadn't used her teeth. "I figure you're private," she said. "That's okay, lotsa friends went private. Good guys. Most of them."

"I'm working on a case involving the woman who rented apartment seven-twenty," I told her.

"What's the case?" she asked.

"I'm not sure," I said. "She came to me to find her brother. I found him. Next day he's dead and I can't find her. I track down her phone number and it leads to apartment seven-twenty upstairs. An empty apartment except for a phone machine."

"You think this babe did her own brother?"

"I would sure like to at least ask her that question."

She laughed. "I like the way you put that. Just like Marty. Hell, always talking about going private. Set up his own operation. He isn't gonna be no square badge long as I'm around. If he was goin' to quit the force, then he'd be home nights. Get any job he wants, only he can't carry a gun anymore and gotta be home nights."

"He's still on the force?"

"He died six years ago." She drank from her beer. "What do you want to know about the tenant in seven-twenty?"

I stared at her, then said, "What can you tell me?"

She opened the file. "Wanted to rent the place for one month. I told her we don't rent for less than three months, two months in advance. So she pays me three months and tells me I could rent it out again after a month. Paid cash and didn't ask for a receipt." She closed the file. "Case closed," she said.

"What did she look like?"

"You said she came to you for a case. Didn't you look at her?"

"I just wanted to make sure it's the same woman."

She looked at me as she raised the beer bottle to her lips and took a languorous pull. "You know, I said that privates were okay in my book, but I didn't mean that I gave them everything they want for free. If you know what I mean."

I took out my wallet and laid a twenty-dollar bill on the yellow Formica tabletop. She looked down at the bill. "Didn't you hear about inflation?"

I laid another twenty on top of the first one. She looked down at the bills, then up at me with expectant eyes. I shook my head. She grabbed the bills and stuffed them into the pocket of her robe. "No use being greedy, I suppose," she said. "Now, what do you want to know?"

"What did she look like?"

"Usual," she said.

"Usual what?" I asked.

"Usual Hollywood-type babe."

"You mean glamorous?" I said, feeling my brow furrow.

"Yeah. You know, diamond bracelet, diamond rings. Probably got diamonds on her nipples." She laughed. "Couldn't see much more than the diamonds, though. She had on a big floppy hat and dark sunglasses and a scarf came up to her chin.

Maybe she was a TV star. I don't know, don't watch that crap. Don't even have a set. Radio's all I need. Whoever she was, she didn't want me knowin' it. And for three months rent in tax-free cash for one month's occupancy—that's fine by me. Do that deal all day long."

"What name did she give you?"

"Never gave me one. Like I told you, she paid me in cash and didn't ask for a receipt. What did I care what her name was?"

I was starting to hear that rushing noise that comes when things won't hold together the way they should. "Listen, how about a woman of medium height, Midwest plain-looking, pale lips, mousy hair, muddy brown eyes?"□

She looked at me. "How about what?"

"Could that have been her?"

"Not in a million years, fella."

"What else?" I asked.

"Nothin' else. That's it. A Hollywood society babe dripping with diamonds comes and rents an apartment in this neighborhood. I figured she was going to use the place to screw her chauffeur."

"Did you ever see her again?"

She wrinkled her nose and furrowed her brow. "Don't think that I did. But that's not unusual—I don't see much of any of the tenants here."

"No phone number or address or any information on her?"

"Not a thing."

"Can I see the folder?"

"You're a paying customer," she said and slid

the stained folder across the table to me.

I looked through the papers inside. There was nothing of use to me. I closed the folder and slid it back to her.

"Sorry, Shamus," she said, "but you pays your money and you takes your chances. That's all the information I got to sell you."

I stared at her. Her eyes said she had told me the truth. "Thank you," I said, getting up.

"Glad to be of help," she said. "And listen, take any of my trinkets you like. Grab a silver crucifix out of a cigar box, or nab one of the dashboard Christophers."

I took one of the Christophers out of sympathy for his recent fall from grace.

From a payphone, I called L.A. Parker Center and was lucky enough to catch Harvey Moss in. He told me to come right down and say hello.☐

When I entered that great breadbox on stilts, L.A. Parker Center, I had stupidly forgotten about the Colt under my coat and set off an explosion of alarms and was instantly surrounded by half a dozen drawn weapons. When I was allowed to bring my hands down, I showed my permit and the weapon in question and was immediately relieved of both.

Harvey Moss's office was pristine: a clean and polished desk, a window looking out to the smog drifting by, a wall full of handshakes and bright toothy smiles, and a picture of his wife and three kids in a gilded frame.

"Been some time, Frank," he said from across his wide desk.

"Right now, Harvey, everything seems to have been a long time."

He smiled, his L. A. tan wrinkling a little and his blue eyes glistening. "How's life up in Baghdad by the Bay?"

"As confusedly fucked up as ever."

He nodded, and I wondered if the full head of rich blond hair was a wig. "Same as down here. What can I do for you?"

"You recommended a client to me."

"I did?"

"Yeah. A week or so back she showed up at my office with your card. She said you referred her to me."

He looked at me with grave intensity. I didn't remember his eyes that blue, in fact, I didn't remember them as blue at all. He slowly shook his head. "Must have been somebody else."

"She had your card."

"I give out cards all the time."

"You do?"

He nodded.

"Tell me, Harvey," I said, looking around the room for some evidence of a caseload. "Exactly what division are you in?"

He smiled again, a little sheepishly. "We like to refer to it as Strategic Liaison."

"What the hell is that?"

"The movies," he said, and it all started to make sense.

"You handle public relations with the movies."

"Something like that."

"So you go to a lot of press briefings, previews, premiers."

He nodded, then smiled. "Somebody's gotta do it."

I smiled back at him. "Okay, then at one of these affairs, as you were handing out cards like candy to kids, you gave some woman your card and told her to look me up to handle her case."

"This woman—what did she look like?"

"Doesn't matter, because I think she may have been in disguise when I saw her."

"What was the disguise?"

"A Midwestern spinster looking for her long lost brother."

He shook his head slowly. "Don't think I'd run across someone like that in the venues I'm involved in."

"How about a woman dripping with diamonds and a big hat and a fancy, expensive scarf?"

"Here in L.A.? Whoever could that be? What's your big interest in all this?"

"Whoever this person is she's murdered someone and set me as a patsy for it."

He whistled. "And you think I may have had something to do with getting her on to you?"

"All I can say is she showed me your card."

"I wish I could be of help. Maybe she found one of my cards tossed in the street after some big gathering."

He was probably right. I could think of no

reason he wouldn't be honest and direct with me. I got up. "I've taken up enough of your time, Harvey. It was just a lead I needed to check out."

"Sure, Frank. Sure. And I have to be off to a meeting out at Studio City. Nice of you to stop by."

"Yeah," I said. "Nice to see you, Harvey."□

It took me nearly an hour of forms and procedures to get my license and gun back.

It was after midnight when I got back from L.A. I was so exhausted, even the couch sounded good. When I opened the door, I stopped in the doorway. There was someone laying on the couch. I took out the Colt. "Okay," I said.

"Frank?"

"Sam? What are you doing here?" Holstering the gun, I went for the light switch.

"Don't turn it on!" she said.

"What's the matter?"

"Please. Don't turn on the light."

I walked through the darkness toward her. "Don't come any closer," she said.

"Sam, what is it?"

"Don't sit on the couch. Stay behind your desk."

I sat at my desk. "Sam, what's the matter?"

"I'm all right," she said, her voice quavery. "I'm just a little bruised up."

"Terry?"

"Please, Frank, he didn't mean to."

I jumped up. "Godammit, where is he?"

"Please, Frank, don't make it worse. Sit down.

You can't help."

I sat down and poured a drink from the bottle left sitting on the desk. "I told you not to go back to him," I said.

"I know. I know, you told me. People are always telling me things. I'm a bad girl, Frank."

Her voice didn't sound right, as if it was coming from a transcription. "Have you been to a doctor, Sam?"

"I'm going to see Dr. Tompkins in the morning."

"Who's Dr. Tompkins?"

"My psychiatrist."

"You're going to a psychiatrist?"

"He's all that's holding me together these days, Frank."

She was backlit by the dim yellow light from the window and I couldn't make out any of her features. "When did you start going to a psychiatrist?"

"I think a very long time ago," she said dreamily.

"Why?"

"Because of what people are trying to do to me."

I wanted to see her face; her words weren't making any sense. "What people are trying to do what to you?"

"Frank, you don't know the kind of enemies I have."

"Enemies?"

"A world full, Frank."

"You're not making any sense, Sam. Go back to the beginning and tell me about it."

She sat silent in the dark. I could see her hands moving in her lap, two black snakes wrestling. "Beginning?" she finally said. "I can't remember anymore where the beginning is."

"Why are you going to Dr. Tompkins tomorrow?"

"He has to adjust my medication."

"What medication?"

"I'm only on it for a little while. Until people stop doing things to me."

"Am I doing things to you?"

"Not yet."

"What will I do to you?"

"Don't, Frank. Don't tease me. You're all I have left."

"From what?"

"I told you, I don't know. People are just doing things to me behind my back."

"Terry? Is Terry doing things to you?"

"I've been shielding him. He's weak."

"Why did he beat you up, then?"

"He's just an innocent bystander. He doesn't know anything that's going on."

"Does he know you're going to a psychiatrist?"

"He mustn't find out!"

I poured another drink and stood up. She turned away as I approached. "Here," I said, "this will help."

She gulped the drink, then let the glass fall and put her hands to her face and sobbed. I sat next to her and pulled her against me.

"I can't find which way is up anymore since I got married, Frank. I don't know how to stop it."

"You have to get away from Terry."

She pulled back and looked into my eyes. I could see her face now: Her cheeks were bruised and puffy. There was a cut across her forehead, blood crusted on it. One lip was split. "It's not Terry," she said.

The hollowness in her voice frightened me. "What do you mean, not Terry? Who did this to you?"

"I did this to me," she said softly, then buried her head in my chest. "You won't say anything to Terry about my coming here, will you?" she said.

"No, I'm just going to quietly beat his brains out and let him guess why."

She trembled against me. "Frank, don't! Don't say anything about this to him. He can't be involved."□

I took her by the shoulders and held her away from me. "Sam, this is screwy. I thought it was Terry that hurt you. If he didn't, tell me who did?"

She put her arms around my neck and smothered me with a kiss. I fell back on the couch. She rolled on top of me. "You're the only safe place for me, Frank. Don't let me lose you, too," she said.

She kissed me with desperation, pulling at my shirt, moaning. I tried to restrain her but she only gave cries of pain when I did.

The fierce primal energy that possessed her

began to flow into me and I encircled her with my arms and pulled us tight together.

I was lying alone on the couch, wearing only socks. The window was open, cold morning air blowing across me. Sam was gone. I got up and went to the green file cabinet to get a towel out of the pile of laundry stuffed in the bottom drawer. I wrapped the towel around me and went down to the bathroom at the end of the hall for a hot shower.

When I got back to the office, I sat at the desk and poured a drink. When that one was finished, I poured another. Between sips, I saw that the glass in my hand trembled. I was drinking before I'd even had breakfast.

I poured the rye back into the bottle and got up and went around the room, picking up socks and shirts and pants. I dug out the tangle of old laundry.

When everything was in a bundle outside the office door, I called the Vietnamese laundry around the corner and told them to come by and put a rush on the order.

I put on sweatshirt and sweat pants and went to get some breakfast.

Back in the office, I re-poured my drink—it was after breakfast now.☐

I wanted to call Terry and grill him about what was going on with Sam, but I'd promised her I wouldn't.

I took out the Yellow Pages and looked up Dr.

Tompkins. His office was high up in the Transamerica Building. I dialed the number.

"Dr. Tompkins' office."

I didn't like her voice—it had that "take-a-seat and wait" lilt. "Let me talk to Dr. Tompkins," I said.

"Who is calling?"

"I want to talk to him about Samantha Healy," I told her.

"Is this an insurance inquiry?"

"No," I said and left it at that.

"Are you the husband or a close relative of the patient?"

She was asking me for a badge, for some proof that I had a right to be concerned about another human being. "A close friend," I said.

"I am afraid Dr. Tompkins is not in at the moment and has quite a full schedule for the day. He may be able to return your call this evening."

I gave her my number and was left with only a dial tone.

I decided to get back to work and wait until the good doctor called. I took out the file on the Orin Hammond case and looked at my notes. They didn't tell me anything.

I started doodling on the inside cover. Who was Eunice Hammond? What was her connection to the diamond-studded L.A. starlet who had rented the apartment in Hollywood? Where did she get Harvey Moss's card? Who killed Cock Robin?

The stick guy stretched his arms out, but couldn't quite get his grip on the stick girl. I made his arms longer, but they still didn't reach.

Pouring myself a drink, I asked myself if maybe I wasn't such a good detective anymore. Maybe I'm too old. Maybe I'm drinking too much. Maybe I'm sliding down the backside of the mountain faster than I know.

I finished the drink and poured another. A few drops came out of the bottle. I tipped it straight up and down and banged the bottom. A few more drops dribbled out and that was it. I dumped the bottle in the wastebasket and went to the top drawer of the green file cabinet. There were no more bottles. I went back to the desk and downed the few drops in the glass. Placing the glass back on the desk, I noticed my hand shaking. My face grew clammy and my throat went dry. For someone who didn't have a drinking problem, I was taking it pretty hard that there was no more liquor in the house.

I grabbed my coat and went out for air. While getting air I stopped in at the liquor store and picked up two quarts of Old Overholt—just in case company stopped by unexpectedly.

When I got back to the office, the same questions were still waiting for me on top of my desk. I poured a drink and lit a cigarette. I looked out the window to the street below. I smoked and drank and looked and waited. Nothing came.

I swung back to the desk and dialed Eunice Hammond's number. The intercept operator came on and said the number had been disconnected with no forwarding. She was out there tying up loose ends. And I was still one of them.

I sat back and stared out the window. Somebody had gone through a lot of trouble to hire me to find Orin so they could murder him—that was clear to me. Was the woman in the Monkey Ward dress just a dupe? Was she behind the case herself? Why?

A fly buzzed languidly by and landed on the window as if he wanted me to notice him. Thinking of insects brought me back to Orin. He was in the porno business. Okay, so then his death had to do with pornography. Maybe he was blackmailing someone who was tired of paying and decided it was cheaper to kill him. Someone like a movie star with lots of diamonds. Who then puts on a big hat and big sunglasses and wraps a big scarf high around her neck so nobody could recognize her and then rents a room to put an answering machine in so I can call and tell her where to find Orin.□

It didn't make a lot of sense. He wasn't hiding. He wasn't hard to find.

There was a knock at the door. My laundry was back. I paid the bill and gave him a tip for the rush delivery, then hung everything on the little rope I kept strung across the back corner of the room.

I returned to my chair and poured a drink and lit a cigarette and thought about the woman who wore lots of diamonds and had big sunglasses—in L.A. That narrowed the field down quite a bit, didn't it?

I picked up the bottle and glass and cigarettes and lighter and went to the couch and lay down to drink and smoke and maybe take a nap and just get away from things for a while.

On the way to the couch, I stopped by the boxes of books still stacked haphazardly since the eviction from my apartment. I picked up Sun Tzu's *The Art of War*. It seemed as good as anything at the moment.

After I'd gotten myself laid out so that my back wasn't complaining, I opened the book at random. "Without deception you cannot carry out strategy, without strategy you cannot control your opponent," Mei Jaochen spoke from two thousand years ago.

I tossed the book across the room. Mei was right, I was being controlled by a strategy based on deception. So far, Eunice Hammond and the diamond lady were better warriors than I was.

I stared up at the ceiling. Now the fly was crawling there—I wondered if it was the same one. I blew smoke at the ceiling. Did the fly think a fire had broken out—did he feel an urge to rush home to see if family and friends were all right? Did a fly have family and friends? Why should he?—I didn't.

I didn't like being controlled by strategy and deception. I was too old and too wise to be pushed around.

Then it began to coalesce. Just like the article I'd read once long ago in Scientific American at the barbershop. My friend the fly up on the ceiling had reminded me. To us, his pattern of motion through the air seemed aimless and chaotic. But if you dabbed a spot of reflective paint on him and filmed his flight, over time very specific patterns arose.

I finished my drink and headed for Eddy's.

It was too early for Eddy to be open, so I went around and banged on the back door.

A dark eye appeared on the other side of the small peephole, then, "My man," Eddy said as he opened the heavy steel door. "What's up?"

"I need to do some thinking and my office is too lonely at the moment," I said.

"Come on in."

He slammed the big door with a heavy clang, and I flinched a little. "Nervous as a blind cat in a fish market," Eddy said.

I followed him through the narrow hallway to the bar. There's something very dank and dismal about an empty bar in the morning. Without the music and laughter and clinking of glasses, you realize it's just a sad, foul-smelling, empty, decaying room—lifeless until its soul returns.□

I took my stool and Eddy took his place behind the bar. "Interest you in a drink, my man?" he said.

I nodded.

"Tough case?" he said as he poured.

"Yeah," I said.

"Sure 'nough nothin' you can't handle."

"Yeah. Nothing I can't handle."

"So give it to me," he said, refilling my glass.

"Few days ago a very plain woman shows up at my office wanting me to find a long lost brother of hers."

"Pretty hard to lose a relative like that."

"She fed me a good fairytale about a divorce, an aunt, a wicked father, with enough twists and turns to keep me following where she was leading."

"Uh-huh. Trouble right there—man starts following a woman where she leads him, you know it ain't gonna turn out good."

"I should have paid more attention. But at that moment a thousand dollar retainer was what I was concentrating on."

"Makes sense."

"I find the brother pretty easy."

"Case not closed though."

"Exactly. I find him and the next day he's dead."

"And you think ain't no coincidence."

"Right."

"Who's this guy anyway."

"Local low lifer in the porno business."

"Who isn't these days 'round here. You happen to come across anybody might want to kill him while you was lookin' for him?"

I nodded. "A few."

"Figures. Line of work that can make lotsa enemies. Maybe was a coincidence. Maybe somebody tryin' to move in on his territory. Or maybe he was tryin' to move in on somebody else's."

I shook my head. "It was her."

"The plain lady?"

"The other one."

"What other one?"

"The one who rented an apartment in L.A. just

to place an answering machine on the floor to receive my call about Orin. The one the landlady said was dripping with diamonds and wore a big hat and bunched up scarf so she could hardly see her face."

"You say she rented a place just to put a phone machine in it? Got a phone number to nowhere just so you could call her and tell her where he was."

"Not really. She could have found him as easily as I did."

"Then why did she hire you?"

"To set me up as a patsy for his murder."

"Bad client to have. Why she be wantin' to off her own brother?"

"Good question."

"Maybe a big inheritance and she didn't want to split any of it with nobody. Not even her brother."

"Possible. But why risk it all by murder?"

"People crazy these days. Can't get enough of anything. Specially money. Do anything to get their hands on more and more. Take a chance on hell for another thousand bucks."

"Exactly."

"But what's her connection to the plain lady?"

"I think they're one and the same."

He whistled. "Lordy. Spun like a spider."

I nodded.

"We gotta get you outa this mess, my man."

"That's why I'm here."

"Let me have it and it's yours."

"You have a son-in-law who is a police detective in Oakland, right?"

"That be Amos. Cold bro."

"I could use his help."

"Then you got it. What you need?"

"Call him and tell him I need to talk to him."

The phone was ringing when I got back to my office, and when I picked it up a very soothing voice said, "This is Dr. Tompkins. You placed a call to me regarding Samantha Healy. I'm afraid that I am only able to get back to you now."

He had the kind of voice evangelists and some politicians have, the kind that causes women to get shaky in the knees and overly dependent. "I'm very concerned about Samantha," I told him. "She's been acting strangely lately."

I could almost hear the stifle of a yawn. "What was your name again?" he asked.

"Frank Malory," I told him.

"Ah, yes. . . . " he dangled. "Well, Mr. Malory, it's not unusual for a patient to go through a period of . . . " There was a pause that had the aroma of a superior mind searching for the right word to explain something to the uninitiated. "Well, a period of acclamation, shall we say."

"You've got her on some kind of drug," I said. "What is it?"

"Oh, I'm afraid I can't discuss that without written authorization from the patient," he said matter-of-factly. "But I can tell you that you need not be worried. Any problems are usually ironed out as we adjust the dosage."

I realized that I shouldn't have answered the call, I was in no mood to deal with a guy like this. "Listen, this woman is going off the deep end and it's due to whatever it is you're dealing. You'd better listen to me. Stop giving her whatever you've got her on or I'm going to come over there and break your prescription-writing fingers one at a time."

There was silence on the line. I could tell he wasn't yawning anymore. "Perhaps you, too, should be seeking professional help, Mr. Malory. That was quite an outburst of hostility we just experienced, wasn't it?"

"Are you going to tell me what you've got her on or not?" I pressed.

"I am afraid that I cannot bend my professional standards under any circumstances, Mr. Malory."

"I'll tell you what you can do with your 'professional standards'—" The line went dead in my ear. "Shit," I yelled at the phone and slammed it down.

I lit a cigarette and poured a drink and yelled, "Shit" again.

I called Sam's, hoping Terry would answer so I could talk to him about it. I only got the answering machine. I left a message for Terry to call me. Then I poured a drink and went back to the couch to think.

When I woke up, I poured myself a shot of rye and lit a cigarette. I blew smoke into the dim room and watched the dark cloud float to the dark ceiling. I hated the dark. I could feel the Devil in the dark, feel his breath at the back of my neck. Everything bad happens in the dark. I lived my life mostly in the dark—lurking in doorways, watching, waiting to catch people as the Devil does, breathing down the backs of their necks. I should have been a dentist like my mother wanted. Dentists work in the light and sleep in the dark. I should have been a baseball player, like my father wanted. When they play in the night, it's lit up like daytime and there's forty thousand people cheering. The Devil can't even get close.

I got up and switched on the desk lamp. It only sent the shadows to lurk in the corners of the room.

I put on a fresh white shirt and a pressed tie along with a pair of blue gabardine slacks and my gray herringbone blazer and headed for Eddy's.

I hadn't realized it was Friday night. The place was packed, everyone on their feet clapping and stomping to the rhythm of the Dixieland group blazing from the bandstand. I squeezed up to the bar and joined in with the crowd.

As soon as Eddy spotted me, he came over to where I was leaned against the bar. "Tomorrow at four in the afternoon work for you Frank? Meet here with Amos?"

"Yeah," I said. "That's fine."

He smiled. "Whatever you needs, my man. Pretty great band don't you think," he added, pointing at the crowded little bandstand.

"Just what I need, Eddy. Just what I need."

He laughed and poured me a double.

At one-thirty the band finished. The place was still jammed, everybody hollering for more. I rapped my glass on the bar to join the noise. The band obliged with "When the Saints Go Marching In" and the singing and hand clapping and hollering got so loud it almost drowned out the music. It was a great night at Eddy's.

Finally, by two a.m., Eddy had to go up on stage and announce that if there were any more encores, he'd lose his license.

It's a sense I've heard that cats have—they pick it up through their whiskers. It's also one that detectives develop—the ones that survive.

I don't know what it was that tipped me. On the walk back to my office the air was thick with clinging fog that glowed dimly in a weak moon. I'd nearly passed by him: a street person sitting hunched in a doorway, keeping warm under a shabby oversized overcoat—not an unusual sight on my block. But something danced on my whiskers. I lightened my step, listening behind.

Then I heard it and spun around. He was tall, the big overcoat billowing like a cape, a blade in his right hand.

There wasn't time for my gun. I let fly my right foot into his crotch.

He ran right into it and howled like a wounded tiger, but kept coming, the hand with the knife steady.

I spun sideways and felt the blade pierce my arm above the elbow. His hand wrapped around the side of my head mashing my ear.

I tried to rip free, only getting my back against him, his grip too strong. I shoved my right hand under my coat, grabbed the Colt, tilting the holster so it was pointing straight back.

I don't know how many explosions there were—more than one.

The hand on the knife fell away. I waited with my finger on the trigger. His other hand let go. He leaned into me, sagged, then slithered to the ground.

I sank into a sitting position, my chin sagging against my chest. The fog collected on the tip of my nose. I breathed fast shallow breaths. There was a noise. I pulled out the Colt. He might have an accomplice. The tip of the barrel hit against something. I looked down. The knife was still sticking out of my arm.

Something was out there. I tried to see through the shimmering grayness. There was the shuffling sound of uncertain feet, then footsteps running away.

I laid the gun in my lap and grabbed the knife and jerked it out, letting it clatter to the sidewalk. With my right hand I undid my tie for a tourniquet.

I made the half block to the street door of my building.

Climbing the stairs, I stopped to catch my breath every other step. There was a lot of blood on the sleeve of my coat, despite the tourniquet.

Inside the office I collapsed into my chair. I took the bottle of Old Overholt sitting on the desk and drank.

I picked up the phone and dialed the Mission District precinct. "Let me talk to Escobar."

"Lieutenant Escobar is not in."

"Where is he?"

"Who is this?"

"Frank Malory."

"This is Johnson, Frank. Escobar is riding patrol with a new rookie unit. He'll be on the road his entire shift."

"Can't you radio him?"

"If it's not important, he'll chew my ass."

"There's been a mugging."

"I don't think he'd want to roll his unit on that. Let me dispatch someone in the area. Where'd it take place?"

"I think Escobar will be interested. The perpetrator got blown away by the victim."

"A homicide?"

"Justified," I said.

"Okay, give me the details and I'll radio Escobar."

I told him what had happened and gave him the location where they could find the body and told him the address of my office where they could find me.

After hanging up, I started to pour, but had to set the bottle down and go over to the sink and stick my head under the faucet.

I took off my coat and examined the charred hole in the back of it, then laid it across the desk. I pulled the Colt from its holster and set it on top of the coat.

It wasn't until the third shot of rye that I started to calm down.

I was lighting a cigarette off the butt of the one I'd just finished, when I heard the siren. Pretty slow response for a homicide. Joe must have been at a Doggy Diner, telling the rookies how wonderfully exciting the old days had been.

10

Lieutenant Joseph Escobar was from Cuba. His father had run a nightclub before the revolution, then had done well in this country for the same employers in Las Vegas. Of the eight kids he'd produced, only one was a scowling ascetic cursed with the burning ambition to grow up and become a police detective. I had still been on the force when Joe started and helped him as much as I could.

He didn't bother knocking, just casually opened and came in, telling the two uniforms accompanying him to wait outside the door. "You look like hell, Frank. What happened?"

He was short and dark-skinned, with black straight hair and had small, very dark, passionless eyes that stared out at the world as if they could never quite believe what they were seeing. "Some guy with a knife jumped me. We struggled. I shot him," I said.

He stood motionless, staring, his lips pursing, as if he'd just pressed a lemon to them. "Why would he do that, Frank?" he finally said.

"Hell if I know," I said.

He wore a dark blue suit and crisp white shirt and a bright red silk power tie under his London Fog belted trench coat. He looked more like a banker than a cop. "It doesn't add, Frank," he said.

"Want a shot?" I asked, holding up the bottle of Old Overholt.

"Okay," he said.

I poured some rye into the pony glass and shoved it across the desk. "Thanks," he said. The arm of his raincoat made a crinkling sound as he downed the drink.

He gave a small grimace. "Rough stuff," he pronounced.

"An acquired taste," I told him.

He set his glass on the desk, and I made a move toward it with the bottle, but he waved his hand over the glass. "I still have a night's work to do."

I pulled the glass to my side of the desk and refilled it. "Is he dead?" I asked.

"The medical examiner's on the way, but I won't need him to tell me. What were you doing out on the street that time of night?"

"Going home from Eddy's."

"Where's the knife?" he asked, training his dark eyes on mine.

"Back at the scene," I told him, wondering what he was getting at.

"The report you called in said he knifed you."

"That's right."

"No knife at the scene, Frank."

"I pulled it out of my arm and let it fall on the sidewalk not two feet from the body."

"Where's the wound?"

I swung in the chair so my left arm came into the light. "You must have a pint of blood spilled out of that arm, Frank. I called for medics. That should be them," he said to the sound of a siren pulling up.

I swung the chair back and downed the drink in my glass. "Did your guys look for the knife?"

He went to the door and opened it. "Chin," he said to the officer on the right of the door, "radio back to O'Reilly at the scene and tell him to look again for a knife. On the sidewalk. Near the body."

He closed the door and came back and stood in front of the desk. "I don't think there is any knife, Frank."

"Maybe some bum came along and found it before you got there. Or maybe there was a second party to the attack. I heard footsteps. Sounded like a small guy."

"Doesn't add up to a mugging, does it, Frank? Who mugs a guy your size? Did he say anything?"

"No."

"I can waste a lot of time trying to find out what really went down, Frank."

"I wish there was something more I could tell you, Joe."

The door opened and one of the uniformed officers looked in. "Paramedic's here."

Joe nodded.

He was tall and lean, his hair tied back in a long ponytail. He looked to Joe who flashed a glance toward me. I wrested my arm on the desk and he came to look. "This should go to an emergency room. You're going to need blood."

"You can handle it," I told him. "You saw a lot worse in Vietnam."

He looked up at me. "I was fourteen when that war ended."

"Do what you can; it's never as bad as it looks."

He opened his black bag and took out a pair of surgical scissors and cut away the blood-soaked sleeve. "He's right," Joe said. "You should go to the hospital for that."

"I had a friend who went to the hospital once—"

"I know, he never came back," Joe finished for me.

The door opened and a short, squat, half-bald man lugging a large black case came in. He looked at Joe. "Guy behind the desk," Joe said. "Paraffin test."

The evidence man set his case on the desk and opened its wide top. He started to reach for my hand. "No way," the paramedic said. "This guy's not moving a muscle until I'm through."

"It's nice to be in demand," I said, then yelped when he poked my arm.

"I hit you with a topical, but it's still going to hurt." He turned to the evidence man. "I've got some stitching to do."

The evidence man looked at Joe, who said,

"Go on down to the scene. He's already admitted he fired the weapon."

The evidence man locked up his case and ran his hand twice over his half-bald head, then left.

"That the gun?" Joe said.

"Yeah," I told him through gritted teeth.

He took out a starched white handkerchief and picked up the Colt by its barrel. "This thing's older than me, Frank." He smiled, pleased with himself. "Hell, it's almost older than you." He smiled again.

"They don't make them like that anymore," I said.

"I'd hate to have to lug this around all day. This the coat you fired it through?"

I nodded as I fought back the pain. "Almost done," the paramedic said.

Joe held up the coat in front of him. "A .45 really blasts the powder out, doesn't it, Frank?" he said.

I nodded.

He dropped the coat back to the desk. "Well, I'll do the best I can for you on this. I hope to hell you're not holding back anything." He carefully refolded his handkerchief and returned it to its pocket and left.

The paramedic finally finished his stitches and wrapped my arm tight with a heavy gauze pack. "It's going to hurt like hell when the topical wears off. I'll leave you some codeine, but you should get to your physician for a prescription. If it bleeds a lot through the packing you're going to need surgery. Maybe it just nicked the artery and the packing will hold it until it heals itself. But maybe not, so watch for too much blood coming through. "

11

I was on the couch half asleep trying to figure out the attack when I heard the door open, reminding me again that I needed to get that damn lock fixed. I was reaching for the Colt when I saw that it was Rita.

She looked quickly around the room. "It looks terrible."

"Not so bad."

"There's blood. My God—your desk and chair. That coat has a big burned spot."

I nodded and raised up on the couch, groaning from my injured arm. "What time is it?"

"Noon. And that bandage needs to be changed."

"I'll get to it."

She put the cardboard tray on the desk. "Do you have fresh wrapping?"

"Don't worry about it."

She stared at me with those deep dark eyes and I tried to look away. She said, "You don't want me worrying about you, do you?"

"I'm not a good person for anyone to worry about. But you could hand me one of those coffees."

She brought me a coffee and stood staring down at me. "I came to tell you I'm leaving. To say goodbye and thanks."

"For what?"

She shook her head. "Just thanks."

"Where?"

"I'm going to get into my Avian and fly to Nairobi with a tank of oxygen."

"Don't you mean Nungwe?"

She looked at me in silence. "What?" I said to her intensity.

"You've read her? West With The Night? Beryl Markham?"

I indicated the box of books in the corner. "She's in there with Out of Africa and all."

She went toward the chair, then looked down at the dried blood and leaned against the desk instead. She took the lid off the other coffee and sipped thoughtfully. Then she picked up one of the doughnuts and handed it to me.

"Maybe you saw my copy that night," she said, more to herself than to me.

"I read lots of different books," I said.

She looked at me, and I looked away. She said, "Why do I have to go?"

"I'm sure it's for the best."

"You're being patronizing."

"Yeah," I said, my mouth full of doughnut.

"Can a black man marry a white woman? A white woman marry a black man? It's nothing more than a prejudice."

"If I understand what you're getting at, I think it's a justifiable one."

She looked at me with eyes that could steam water. "Frank! Do you have any idea what men my age are like? Shallow. Stupid. Greedy. Dumb as a dog."

"Look," I said, "I'm no Denis Fitzhatten. And I've had someone who worried about me, once. I don't want to go through that loss again."

"What happened to her?"

I tossed the rest of the doughnut into the wastebasket. "A long story."

The phone rang and we looked at each other a long moment and then I got off the couch and picked up the phone.

"Frank, here," I said into the receiver.

"It's Joe, Frank."

"Yeah, Joe."

"Your arm turn green yet?"

"Just a light shade of chartreuse."

"It wasn't a mugging, Frank."

I leaned against the desk next to Rita. "What do you mean?"

"Got the report on the guy you shot. No mugger."

"Who was he?"

"Maybe you should come down to the station. Answer some questions."

"I've got a date."

"I thought you might want to fill out a new report."

"What I told you is how it happened. There's no more to say. If the DA's office can't swallow it, that's their problem."□

"Doesn't add, Frank."

"Why not? Who was the guy?"

"Name was Christopher Wolfe. That mean anything?"

"No."

"Latest residence was L.A. Worked down there as a stunt man in the movies. Previous to that he was hanging out in San Salvador. Got a bad history."

There was silence on the line. "Go on," I said.

"Doesn't add, Frank. Guy like that doesn't hang around Mission Street mugging people."

Banks of fog began slowly burning away inside my head. "If you've got a prosecutor who doesn't like my story, you can bring me in and I'll repeat it to his face. So long, Joe," I said.

"What was all that?" Rita said.

"The case I'm working on."

"About the man who stabbed you?"

"No, about the woman who sent him."

She stared at me with an uncertain look. "Listen," I said, "I've got to go to L.A."

"I understand," she said, turning from me. "I'll go away."

I grabbed her arm. "No, I didn't mean it that way. It's about this case. I want you to wait for me to come back."

I was stuffing some extra clothes and the two bottles of Old Overholt into a laundry bag for a carry on when the phone rang.

I figured it was probably Escobar trying again to get me to come in. I was halfway to the door when I decided to tell him off and swung back and picked up the receiver. "Yeah," I said.

"That you, Frank?"

"Harvey?"

"Yeah."

"What's up?"

"I have been talking with some of the guys up there in San Francisco. Sounds as if you have been snagged into a phony frame and you have Homes on your back over in Oakland."

"You are exactly right."

"That son of a bitch Homes is in on the frame as far as I'm concerned. It was most likely a hit set up by some of his guys. They are all crazy no good sons of bitches up there. I know that. Hell, I would be chief of police in San Francisco today if it hadn't been for that fucking rat."

"It wasn't Homes who set it up. It was my client."

"The one in the Plain Jane outfit looking for her brother?"□

"That's right."

"I have been thinking about that also. There is another woman, you said. Someone with big sunglasses and a big scarf."

"That's what the landlady told me. Between the

hat, glasses and bunched up scarf she couldn't make out her face."

"Well, for some reason, the idea of the big scarf stuck in my mind. After all, who wears big scarves anymore. Sort of an Isadora Duncan thing, right? You know about Isadora Duncan, don't you?"

"I've come across her in biographies."

"The woman loved scarves. Danced in them. Wore them. They were her brand identification. And they did her in. She was riding with this Italian mechanic she just met named Falchetto. He had this crazy sports car. Amilcar roadster it was called. A kind of an open racing car of the twenties that you could drive on the street also. The damn thing had virtual bicycle wheels, nothing but open spokes. And the passenger seat was only a few feet from the rear wheel. You know how I know all this?"

"How?"

"Just last week, I met with Richardson, the director. He has obtained development money for a script for a biopic on Duncan and came to me regarding clearances for some street scenes in Venice that he may put into the script. He would intend to make it look like Paris of the twenties. Anyway, Duncan hopped into that crazy car to head for her hotel with the Italian mechanic, waving goodbye to her friends, telling them she's off to make love. Then as he roars away she throws her big red scarf across her neck. The scarf keeps going in the wind, snags against the rear wheel, wraps into the spokes, snaps her neck and tosses her out of the car onto the street dragging behind. Makes you think, doesn't it? Let me tell you, I took my tie off on the drive back to the station after lunch."

"And this connects to my case somehow?"

"Just listen to me. I have to be real careful here. I move amongst these people, these movie people, some of the vilest human beings on our planet. But I also need to shove something up Home's ass to get even for what he did to me. And if I can bust up some kind of frame he is running on you, rest assured I am going to do just that.

"Alright."

"So bear with me. I may be trying to tell you something important to your case. I don't know. But it has got to come out in idle chitchat, you understand? You cannot connect me directly with any of this."

"I understand."

"So, I am sitting at lunch with Richardson and he is showing me some items from his research folder. He has a picture of the kind of car. Most think it was a Bugatti, but that's wrong. I think she called the guy, that Falchetto, Mr. Bugatti. Anyway, Richardson brings out an eight by ten of this long scarf. Red silk. And for some reason right at that moment, I think of what you told me, about a woman with big sunglasses and a big scarf. I don't know why but it just flashed through my mind when I saw the photo. You following all this?"□

"Not much."

"All right, let's cut to the chase scene. I ask Richardson where he got the photo of the scarf, and he tells me that he not only has the photo, but access to the scarf itself, and he plans on using it in the film."

"Who has the scarf?"

"That is what I am getting at. And it is more than the scarf. What you told me as to how that landlady described the woman, and about the phone answering machine in an empty apartment—all really fit someone down here in the business."

"Who?"

"Dorothy Desmond. Certainly, you have heard of her?"□

"No."

"Well, you probably don't watch much prime time soap operas. She is a giant TV star on a show that has been going for over eight seasons. And, you know, if you can star in a five-season run you are financially set for life, so she is a pretty powerful figure in the business. But she is aging. And, as they say around here, 'politicians, ugly buildings and madams all get respect as they age'— but not starlets."□

"And you added all this up from seeing a photo of a scarf?"

There was silence on the line. "Alright. I guess you are still too good a detective to know when someone is holding back."

"Let's have it."

"Remember, you told me she came to you with

my card."

"Yes."

"Okay. It was at a press event. We were talking about the business when she suddenly pulled out a yellow page torn from a San Francisco phonebook. She knew I had been on the force up there before I came to L.A."☐

"A page of detective listings?"

"That's right. She said she needed someone to check out some threatening mail she was getting that was postmarked out of San Francisco. She wanted a recommendation from me."

"And you told her to get in touch with me?"

Silence on the line. "Now, understand me, Frank. You know how word travels. I knew the troubles you had been having. You know, that woman who was killed, the business with your wife. Drinking. I was surprised you even still had an ad in the book."

"I paid for three years upfront, so I guess it's still been running. I never check. So you didn't recommend me, then?"☐

"That's right."

"How much didn't you recommend me?"

"Like I said, Frank, you were known to be in rough shape. Probably didn't need a client like her anyway."

"Harvey, this is important. How much didn't you recommend me?"

"You're right, this is the key. The scarf business was just a cover for me. I didn't want this to get personal."

"Never mind about that. Just tell me."

"I guess I told her you were the last detective I would ever recommend she get in touch with."

"That I was a down and out drunk."

"Something like that."

"Someone who she would think could probably be easily fooled into doing anything."

"I suppose."

"And she's an actress. She could make herself up so her own mother wouldn't recognize her."

"No doubt."

"How do I get to her?"

"Now, let's be careful here. As I have said, I've got to move amongst these people. And if you get to her, what are you going to do?"

"I'll work that out as it comes. I just want to I.D. her."

"Well, it will throw a wrench into Home's case at least. Okay, here is how we can do it and keep me out of it. The studio owns a hotel near the production lot where they put up exhibitors who are brought in for a tour. I can knock over some dominoes that will leave no trace back to me. You will be an exhibitor from San Francisco who won some campaign for the most popcorn sales or something. You will be on VIP status and put up in the hotel and taken on a tour of the studio. Just tell them you are a fan of Dorothy Desmond and you will get on her set close enough to make her. Then it's your case from there."□

"Fair enough. I appreciate this, Harvey."

"Just spoil something with Home, that's all I

care about. You should get a call from the publicity department within the hour. Stay by your phone."

We hung up and as far as I was concerned, that locked it up. A simple case, really. A big star gets blackmailed by a low-lifer for some porno reel she did way back when she was trying to get into acting. Then she decides it's safer and cheaper to kill off the blackmailer. So she locates a down and out detective for a patsy, puts herself into a character as far as possible from her real character. Then gets herself a smart little small-caliber revolver fitted with a silencer and shows up for the exchange of money for an old black and white reel that she wants burnt forever. But there may be others. There may be copies. This might not be the end of his control over her. I can just see Orin getting up to reach for the cash and hear the soft thunks of the silencer. As he falls back onto the bed, she takes the film and runs out to that black Mercedes I had seen parked outside. She had probably already called me for help so I would be on my way over. Me—the patsy. She knew once I couldn't find her at the payphone by the liquor store that I'd come to where Orin was staying, and she used that car phone antenna sticking above the back window of the Mercedes to call in the police for sounds of gunshots at Orin's address.☐

But I guess her frame didn't seem tight enough when I was back out on the street so quickly, so she brought in a hit man for that stabbing to get rid of me for good. Those must have been her footsteps I heard in the mist. She was overseeing the job. That's why the knife was never found. She ran up and grabbed it after I'd stumbled off.

So, what was I going to do? I didn't give a damn. I wanted her. Maybe if I could get within two feet of her I'd just reach out and strangle her. Her type could slip through any legal trial. Maybe I could break into her house and find that little automatic with her fingerprints still on it for ballistics to connect her to Orin's shooting.

I got one of the bottles of Old Overholt out of my laundry bag luggage and poured a drink while I waited for the phone to ring.

12

I must have dozed off and when the phone rang I jerked awake in my chair, spilling the drink perched on my chest.

"Mr. Malory, please."

"Yeah."

"Is this Mr. Malory?"

"It is."

"Phillips here, Mr. Malory. From Public Relations. How are you, sir?"

"Is this about the trip to L.A. and the studio?"

"It certainly is. I am calling you to announce that you are one of our VIP winners for—"

"The popcorn contest," I said.

"Popcorn?"

"Yeah. Popcorn."

"Well, that's certainly something to be proud of then, isn't it?"

"So how does this work? How do I get on Dorothy Desmond's lot?"

"Well, to start with, we are going to fly you to

Hollywood at our expense, for a complementary dinner and a night's stay at our wonderful hotel, followed by a fabulous tour of the studios."

"When?"

"Well, it says right here that we are sending a private limousine to take you to SFO this very evening, if you are ready for your trip."

"I'm ready."

"Then if you would just give me your address, you will be contacted by the limousine company for an exact time."

"Life is pretty easy if you sell a lot of popcorn, isn't it?"

There was hesitation on the line, then, "Well, yes, I guess so."

I hung up and refilled my drink, and before I could finish it, the limo driver called. He was concerned about the area of my address, and I told him this was the factory where we made all that prize-winning popcorn, and he seemed to understand. I told him I was upstairs and to honk his horn when he was out front. He explained he had a car phone and would call me when he arrived, which would be soon.

He was standing stiffly by the long limousine and pulled the rear door open as I approached. I tossed in my laundry bag luggage and went around to the passenger door on the front.

"You don't like the back?" he said as we pulled from the curb.

I looked behind me through the glass divider at

what seemed a padded tunnel with seats. "Who needs all that?" I said.

"You'd be surprised."

"Something to make unimportant people feel important."

He nodded. "And a lot of prom kids who throw up all over the seats."

After I'd checked in, the desk clerk called for a bellhop, and when he came I held up my laundry bag for him to take, then asked for directions to the bar.

The bar room was filled with women with large breasts and tight dresses and men with fat cigars and lots of chins. I asked the bartender for an Old Overholt straight and he didn't know what I was talking about. "Make it Scotch, then," I told him. "Single malt. Glenlivit if you have it. Double. No ice."

The bartender came back and set a very shiny crystal glass on the bar before me. I gave him my room number and he nodded, then said, "You here for Dorothy Desmond?"

I stared at him. "What?" I said.

"Tomorrow's the last day of shooting on her series. That's a big day in this town."

"How so?"

"You're really not here about her?"

I shook my head. He pointed out into the crowded room. "Everybody else is."

"I still don't understand," I said. "Who are all these people?"

"The movers and shakers that keep this industry moving and shaking."

"Movie stars?"

"No. They all hang out at the high profile places, pretending not to want their pictures taken. These people here are the real masters of the universe. I thought for sure you were one of them."

"No way."

"I would have said you were an American representative of European money sources."

I laughed. "Why that?"

"Your sport coat is rumpled and there's a stain on your tie. That means you spend time in France. But you don't have a French accent. So you bridge between European money and the industry here."

"Just a guy who sells a lot of popcorn," I said.

He looked at me quizzically. I said, "Tell me more about Dorothy Desmond. She's a pretty big deal down here?"

"Lots of power. Star power. That's what these guys buy and sell."

"They're here to see her."

"In a way. It's big news that her series is over. Mainly because the money people think she's too old for the part, and wouldn't renew her contract. She's let it be known that she's going to be setting up her own studio. Everyone wants in on a piece of the ground floor of that action." He picked up my empty glass. "Another?"

I nodded.

When he came back with the drink it wasn't quite as full as the first one. He leaned against the bar, staring out into the room. "But there's trouble on the horizon already," he said.

"How's that?"

"Buzz going around town about some sort of scandal involving her."

"Regarding what?"

"Just rumors about something that's about to break."

I thought about Orin. It looked like she'd stopped the scandal before it got started. I finished the Scotch and thanked him then left.

I awoke to nothingness. I didn't recognize the room, didn't know where I was, who I was. I felt like screaming but nothing would come out my mouth. I was paralyzed—a toad in aspic.

Finally, I was able to focus on the sound of a phone ringing. With a snap, I came back to myself. Everything rushed in and I sat up in the bed trembling and sweaty.☐

I reached the phone on the nightstand. "Yeah," I said.☐

"Mr. Malory?"

"Who's this?"

"Is this Mr. Malory?"

"Yes."

"This is Mr. Scheinbloom with the studio. Monte Scheinbloom. I'm calling about your tour." The voice was high and fluty.

I ran my hand through my hair and turned away from the phone and coughed. I saw cigarettes and a lighter on the nightstand. "Yeah. Just a minute, Marty," I said. As I put the phone down, I heard his voice squeak over the phone, "It's Monte, not Marty."

When I had the cigarette lighted I picked up the phone. "So what's the deal, Monte?"

"I can come by the hotel in about an hour to pick you up and take you to the studio. How would that work for you?"

"Fine," I said. "I'll wait in the lobby. I'm a representative of European money, so you'll recognize me by my crumpled sport coat and spotted tie."

"Oh?" he squeaked as I hung up.

Monte Scheinbloom looked like his voice sounded; he was tall and willowy. When we pulled up at the guard station at the entrance to the studio a short, squat sentry gave a quick nod to Monte, then came around to my side of the car. He handed me a clipboard and told me to sign at the bottom. "Any firearms or other weapons?" he asked me as I handed him back the clipboard.

"I'm a private detective, licensed to carry," I told him.

"Not in here," he said. "Turn it over."

I looked at him for a moment, then shrugged and pulled the Colt from its shoulder holster. "You'll get it back when you leave," he said and I nodded.

Monte stared at me. "I thought you were an exhibitor from San Francisco."

"Tough crowds up there," I said.

He stared a few beats longer, then took a breath and put the Mercedes in gear and we entered the lot.

The sound stage was crowded—some of the men I had seen in the bar the previous night milling about. Tables were set around with bottles of champagne cooling in silver buckets and caviar in iced servers. On one large table was a four-tiered cake at least five feet tall with images of bright red flapping scarves worked into the frosting.

Monte Scheinbloom maneuvered me through the chattering throng to the edge of the large set of an elaborately decorated living room. Off the stage was a very long trailer with a herd of news reporters and cameramen savagely focused on its door.

"A very exciting day," Monte said.

"I can see."

"She has directed many of the episodes this season, you know."

"That a fact."

"Indeed. Aging won't keep her down. No, she's going to be setting up her own production studio. She'll be in charge. Nothing can stop that woman."

"We'll see."

There was a hush across the crowd as the trailer door flew open. She stood framed in it. I put an overlay on her: blue eyes turned muddy brown by contacts; blonde hair covered by a mousy-colored wig pulled back sternly; all accents of makeup removed; breasts flattened by gauze wrapping like women did in the twenties. And the bright red scarf.

I began moving toward her, staring into her eyes. She didn't see me amidst the camera flashes until I was only a few feet away. Then, her shock was unmistakable. Her hand grabbed at her scarf and she retreated half a step, then stopped. I stopped. We stared.

She whirled so fast the bright red scarf flew out like wings. She rushed into the trailer and slammed the door.

The crowd gasped. I waited.

The trailer door opened and a guy not quite as big as a beer truck came out. He headed straight for me. "Miss Desmond has asked that you be cleared from the set," he said looking down at me, his voice a rumble.

"I need to talk to her first," I said.

He unbuttoned his coat so I could see that the bulge under it wasn't a pack of Kleenex. "We'd better go, now," he said.

I shrugged and said maybe we had.

Outside the sound stage, he grabbed my arm. "Over here."□

I broke his grip and said, "All right, I'm off her set. Now go back and iron a scarf for her."

He grabbed my arm again, this time putting his other hand on the gun under his coat. "I'm to personally escort you off the lot."

"What's with you?" I said, breaking his grip again. "You're going to pull a gun on me for going on a tour of a studio set?"

He pulled the gun out of its holster and held it under his jacket. "This way."

I thought of the Colt back at the guardhouse. Now that I knew she was the one I was looking for I would get to her off the set, so I followed him to a bright red pickup all tricked out with chrome roll bar and beach lights. "Get in."

I shrugged and said, "Okay, I'll get in. But I want you to take me straight to the gate."

We didn't stop at the gate, and they didn't even look up when the red pickup bounded out, obviously a known fixture on the lot. I figured that was okay, once he let me off outside I'd go back for my gun.

But after we had passed through, he tore like a madman into the lanes crowded with traffic.

"What's up?" I said.

He didn't say anything and I began to worry a little. "Where the hell you going? We're off the lot."

He took the gun out with his left hand, a 9mm automatic, and aimed it at my head. "Shut it," was all he said.☐

"Stop and I'll get off here."

He didn't stop. Instead, we roared down the boulevard, the truck bellowing like a dragster as we swerved onto the first freeway on-ramp. We headed east. He kept the gun pointed at me. ☐

I knew he probably wouldn't shoot me on the busy freeway, but the direction we were headed was toward the desert.

We came up on the tail of a car snailing along in the fast lane, and he jammed his hand with the gun on the horn. I grabbed his wrist with both my hands and shoved it upward. The gun fired, tearing a neat little sky blue hole in the roof. The car ahead immediately swerved into the right lane. He tried to lower his arm, but only fired again. He took his hand off the steering wheel and threw a quick awkward punch. I sent it glancing off my jaw. As he grabbed the steering wheel again, I slammed his hand with the gun against the side window. He tried another swing. I blocked it with my elbow.

He brought his knee up under the steering wheel to steady it and grabbed my face with his free hand, feeling for an eye with his thumb. I jerked my head sideways and caught the fleshy part under his thumb between my teeth.

He howled. I spat blood and skin and tried to brain him with his own gun. He grabbed the wheel to keep us from running off the road. I jammed a foot on top of his, slamming the gas pedal to the floor.

The transmission kicked down, the engine roared, the tires screeched, and the souped-up truck leaped forward.

Traffic scampered into the slow lane ahead of us. "Let go the fucking gun or we're going through the sound barrier!" I yelled.

He navigated frantically through the traffic. The speedometer swung past a hundred.

"Let go the fucking gun!" I screamed, trying to shake it loose.

He fired two more rounds through the roof, then jammed a foot on the brake.

The truck slowed. The needle dropped below seventy.

We swerved left as the right front brake disintegrated, shooting us across lanes, cars dodging and honking as we broke through traffic. The speedometer was down to fifty, the engine straining, the brakes howling. He had the truck straightened out, then the left front pad died and we shot ahead again, veering wildly to the right.

His concentration on controlling the truck weakened his gun arm enough that I yanked it down, ramming the top of his head with the gun butt.

The rear brakes gave up their keening as the drums overheated and failed completely. We were heading for a hundred again. I clubbed him again with the gun butt. Blood ran the side of his face. "Drop it! Godammit! Drop it!" I yelled.

The needle had pegged at a hundred and twenty, when I looked up and saw the trucks—two double trailers, one trying to pass the other.

There was a solid line of cars to our right. He dropped the gun. I let go his arm. He grabbed the wheel with both hands and flung us violently to the left.

It was a crumpling explosion. The pops of the airbags going off. The world outside turning blue sky, gray pavement, blue sky, gray pavement. The cab shrunk around me like a balloon deflating.

Everything stopped.

There was the smell of smoldering oil and spilled gasoline.

I was rolled up in a ball under the collapsed airbag.

The smell of gasoline got stronger.

I jammed my feet against what I thought was the door and shoved hard. It didn't give. The truck was on its side and I was pushing against what had been the dash. I rolled and swung my feet above me and shoved. The twisted metal of what had been the door creaked and groaned. I crawled through and tumbled to the ground.

My eyes couldn't focus. There was whooshing of passing cars, distance between them and me.

I wiped at my eyes and then made out the crumple of red that had been the pickup, the bent metal of the door sticking up like a gnarled hand waving to no one.

I struggled up and back to look inside the cab. His body was as twisted as the truck, blood running out his nose and ears. I reached in to try and pull him out, but only my left arm moved. I looked down at my right arm and saw a pointed protrusion just below the elbow. I tried to move my fingers and they didn't.

I reached toward him as far as I could with my left arm.

Then the explosion came.

I was thrown back, skidding across pebble-strewn dirt and banging to a stop sitting against a big boulder.

When I could clear my eyes, I saw the pile of red disappearing into a roar of black smoke.

People were pulling off the freeway and getting

out to stare at the fire.

Something smelled awful.

I wiped my hand across my eyes, then wiped again above them. I didn't seem to have eyebrows anymore.

When I ran my hand over my hair my fingers stung.

A man came rushing at me with a car blanket that he threw over my head as I tried to raise my right hand to push him away.

"You okay?" I heard him say.

I could only hear, not talk.

"That's one hell of a wreck. Good thing you got thrown out. Your hair's on fire."

Maybe why the blanket, I thought.

I pulled the blanket off with my left hand and blinked against the brightness. My Good Samaritan was staring at the still billowing fire. I struggled up and he extended a hand.

A crowd had gathered, like campers watching a bonfire, their cars scattered around the turnout.

I went to one of the cars, a yellow Pinto with its engine still running. I had to reach across with my left hand to put it into gear, my right arm bleeding heavily through the bandage and the pain from the broken bone beginning to pierce my state of shock.

I passed several racing Highway Patrols going the opposite way as I drove back toward Hollywood.

When I got to the studio entrance, the same guard came out with his clipboard. "I just want my gun back," I told him. "Quick."

He stared at me. "What the hell happened to you, fella?"

I swiveled the rearview mirror; I looked like something that had crawled out of hell. "Makeup," I told him. "My final scene. The burning of Atlanta. Now give me the gun."

He huffed a confused laugh and nodded, then went into the guardhouse to come right back out. He snapped a release to the clipboard and told me to sign. I scribbled fast and shoved the clipboard back to him.

He tore off a copy of the form and handed me the pistol. "You even smell like burnt," he said, wrinkling his nose.

I threw the Pinto into reverse and left him scratching his head.

As I drove toward the Hollywood Hills, the closer I got the more stares there were at stoplights. Going down Sunset Boulevard, no one had seemed to think it so strange to see a man driving a yellow Pinto with his eyelashes burned off and his hair a tight singe. The range of what humanity could look like was wider there. Turning onto Beverly and starting the climb into the West Hollywood Hills, homes of the Olympians, I began getting strange looks at stop signs.

I was an alien entering this special land that was anathema to the alien, a land of cultivated sameness, a land where power flowed to those who strove for the purity of Platonic forms. This was the land of those forms, where they arose as if from some sunny mist to be smeared onto celluloid and sent out across all the lands of the earth—the source of human dreams of perfection. This was the seat of the power and wealth that come from purity and sameness, from chasing the single ideal, where all deviations were obliterated so only the ideal remained. And those who achieved its perfection became the rich and the powerful, laws unto themselves, lords of all domains that their rolls of celluloid could reach.

And I had been marked by one of the queens of this land, used as a patsy for her royal ends, part of her disposable world.□

I skidded the car to a stop, threw it into reverse and backed up to the corner where I had seen her. The young girl with long blond hair stared wide-eyed as I reached across the passenger seat and cranked down the window. "Give me one." I struggled to get out my wallet with my left hand. "Hurry!" I said as she just sat there.

Finally, she took one of her maps of the stars' homes off the sagging card table in front of her and came to the car. "How much?" I said.□

"Two dollars." Her voice was weak and shaky. I didn't blame her.

I took a five from my wallet and held it out. She approached cautiously and took the money, then dropped the map onto the passenger seat.

"Keep the change," I said, trying to smile against the pain.

It was the middle of the day and I needed

night, but I wanted to case her place. Following the directions on the map, I wound high up into the Hills, climbing above even the smog line. Like a true Olympian, she lived on the peak of a mountain. The regular road ended and a narrow smoothly paved road began. The yellow Pinto strained up steep stretches. There were clouds, low, almost touching the road in places. At last, there came jacarandas standing in tight, statuesque single file on each side of the road like proud soldiers in purple pomp, then a ten-foot-high stone fence for quarter of a mile to richly scrolled gates. The long smooth road was her private driveway, and its place on the map was only to show gawking tourists that they would get nothing of her private life.□

I pulled the Pinto behind a knoll that shielded it from the road. When the motor was off, I sat and let the pain take hold. I felt injuries all over, the broken arm the worst. There were dark spots on my pant legs. I checked—small gashes, but they had crusted over. The blood had even stopped running on the packing over the knife wound. The broken arm seemed the only danger. I knew the sharp edge of the bone would rub and tear at the skin from the inside, creating an ulcerating wound.

I painfully got my jacket off, then rolled my right sleeve up above my elbow. Carefully loosening my tie, I pulled it over my head, then slipped the loop over my right arm below the elbow where the break was. I slipped the tie carefully into place. I pressed my wrist flat against the gearshift, then passed the end of the tie through the steering wheel and wrapped it around my fist and pulled hard.

My head went light and my vision tunneled, and the screams seemed coming closer, but I managed to keep a steadily increasing pressure. Then I was able to splay the fingers of my right hand a little and, with a pop like the sound of a distant cannon, I felt the bone slip back into place.

I held the tie tight, even though I could see the skin below it all the way to my fingers turning white. Then slowly I released the pull to let the blood flow. The bone stayed in place.

I unwrapped the tie from my fist and pulled it out of the steering wheel, then wound it securely over the break with enough pressure to hold the bone together but not too much to restrict blood flow, then passed the long end around my neck and secured it as a sling.

I worked the pack of cigarettes and lighter out of my shirt pocket.

I finished my cigarette and lit another one. I sat smoking and wondering what I was doing. I needed a drink. I didn't feel myself. Maybe the crash had done something to my head. Maybe it had cleared my head. How do you tell?

I watched the sky through the windshield. Clouds formed and dissolved, like thoughts in my head. Had I chased her here? Or had she chased *me* here? Does a rat know when the cat is chasing him into a corner? Was I the rat or the cat?

I hurt. All over. My feet hurt. My legs hurt. My knees hurt. My stomach hurt. I was hungry. My burnt hair hurt. My singed eyebrows hurt. I was drunk. I was sober. I was a mess of everything.

My ribs hurt under the Colt's holster. I brought the gun out. As much as I hated them, it was reassuring to hold it. I reached to my coat on the floor and took out the two extra magazines and stuffed them into my pants pocket. What did I plan on doing with the gun? Kill myself? Shoot her?

I was drifting away, from the clouds, from myself, from life.

When I awoke it was nearly dark. I had slept the rest of the day away—probably a good idea. I needed a drink to steady myself. I pushed open the Pinto's door and took a deep breath as I held my broken arm gingerly in place and got out.

So far, so good. I crossed the road and went to the gates. They were heavy iron, twelve feet or more tall, two giant D's woven into the frilly design. They were held up by thick pillars.

I took the Colt out and drew its barrel across the iron gate, making a racket to see if there were guard dogs on duty—I hated shooting dogs.

From the gate, past long fields of dark lawn in the dimming light, and down a winding driveway, I could only see the tips of roof peaks against the charcoal sky. From their separations, it looked like a mansion the size I would have expected.

I returned to the Pinto and carefully climbed into the seat to let my weary and damaged bones rest.

I smoked and wondered as I watched the

nightfall—was I Quixote or Parsival?

As the light outside darkened, I saw my reflection in the windshield. It didn't look like me. But how was I to know? It had been so long since I'd had the courage to see myself. A dead wife. A dead client. And now maybe a dead me. And would that such a loss? Because everything I get involved in people get killed. Maybe I am the angel of death. Maybe I'm the one I'm hunting for.

I reached for a bottle. There wasn't any—never a drink when you need one.

I turned away from my reflection and looked out at the tops of the high wall and the tall gates.

It became suddenly clear to me: I had been called here, called to set things right. She had pierced the thin walls that bound the game called civilization. She had decided that it was her right to take whatever she chose at anyone else's expense. And I was the one to bring a stop to it. That was my job. She had made me a patsy, her patsy, and that could not stand. She had called me here at this particular moment, at this particular place. Broken of bone, I was here to set the order back right.

I felt my head slide against the door window as I drifted off.

I jerked awake from lights piercing the dark, pain stabbing my broken arm.

I climbed out of the Pinto and stood watching from the dark behind a tree at the top of the knoll. It was a stretch limousine. I watched the slow, steady operation of the gate openers.

When the limousine had passed through the gates and they'd slowly drawn closed again, I secreted myself behind one of the big pillars. If the limousine was from the studio it would leave after delivering her home, if it didn't come back out there'd be a chauffeur on the grounds to contend with, and I'd have to come up with another scheme to get past the gates.

It wasn't long, though, before shafts of light from the limousine lit the frills of the gate.

The lights stopped. Motors of the gate operators droned. The lights stabbed through, followed by the dark bulk of the limousine. The big car floated silently away. The openers switched gears and I slipped between the slowly closing gates.

The grounds were like a forest. I made my way down from tree to tree until the mansion was in view, lit up like there was a party going on: turrets on the third floor glowing like ship's beacons, the second-floor windows a floating band of suspended yellow swatches and the ground level spilling light onto the jacaranda and wisteria and bougainvillea. Staring at the lights made me dizzy and I had to steady myself against a tree. I needed a drink.□

There was only one window that was black. I headed for it.

I should have known. If I hadn't been so banged up and crazed from it all, I might have.

I carefully felt around the edge of the dark window with my left hand. My fingers found a gap at the bottom sash. I pried into it and lifted. The window slid up. I held my breath and listened. No alarm. I carefully reached inside and felt around the sash. No sensors.

I should have known.

I held my injured arm tight against my chest and swung a leg over the sill. I rested a moment, waiting for the spinning to stop, then clutched my bad arm tight against my chest and ducked and rolled the rest of the way in.

The room was black.

Two steps in, there was a thump at the window. I spun around. I held out my hand and felt the window. There was a cold steel plate over the opening.

I twisted my left arm around and got the Colt out as I dropped to a crouch.

Only silence and blackness.

A cone of light flashed through the room and I spun toward it, swinging the Colt in front of me. The room fell back into blackness. Colored spots danced in my eyes. I sank lower to the floor.

Another flash, then a movie screen on the wall at the end of the room lit with a scratchy black-and-white image aged to a sepia cast. A man sat on a bar stool, looking up at a topless dancer. On the stool next to him was a pneumatic girl in a tight alpaca sweater and what we used to call pedal pushers. "So you think she's got pretty good ones?" she said to him. "Not bad," he answered, his voice gravelly. She took a drink from her glass, "Why don't we go up to my place and I'll show you some real good ones." He looked at her with an amateur lecher stare. "Sure, whatever you say, baby."

I slammed the Colt against the steel plate over the window. It only clattered thickly.

"The room is completely sealed, Mr. Malory," an amplified voice sounded from behind the screen. "You may as well relax and enjoy the show."

I looked at the rows of several dozen plush seats but didn't see her. She must be in the projection room where the shaft of light was coming from.

I looked up at the screen. They were in a dismal bedroom, the man seated on a messed up single bed with a drink in his hand, the girl wearing her slip and bra, dancing for him in the center of the room. She ran her hands sumptuously over her breasts as she writhed out of sync to the blaring music. The man's eyes were riveted on her breasts. "Want to see them?" she said coyly, unsnapping her bra. "They are great!" the man said, his eyes goofy saucers.

"Don't you love the dialogue," her voice came over the speaker. "And not bad tits for a seventeen-year-old in the days before implants."

I studied the woman gyrating on the screen. You could tell it was her—younger but still recognizable as the woman who had stepped out of the trailer, the blue eyes and blond hair coming through even in black-and-white. So it had been what I'd thought.

"You probably think you have it all figured out

now, don't you, Mr. Malory?"

"Probably," I said, pressing tighter against the wall, aiming the Colt at the hole the light came through. "You were a young Hollywood hopeful trying to break in, you needed money and you made a skin flick with Orin Hammond doing the directing."

"Orin Hammond, boy wonder pornographer," she said.

The girl on the screen had all her clothes off now and was working on removing the man's. I went on, wanting to stall while I figured out a plan. "And after you became a big success, you've been afraid someday Orin might show up and try to blackmail you. So you hired me to locate him and then you murder him."

She laughed loudly. "You're hopelessly behind the times, Mr. Detective. The stupid son of a bitch has had this film sitting in a can under his mattress, or wherever, for over thirty years," her voice crackled from the loudspeaker. "He never connected who I was, the stupid little bastard."

"Why did you bother to get the film then?" I yelled. "It sounds like you were safe."

She was silent. I looked up at the screen. The girl had the man undressed and was practicing her womanly arts. "I was pretty good even then," she said softly over the speaker. "I could put a man under my control, let him know who was going to be boss. Such simple creatures."

"Did you just want this film for a stroll down memory lane?" I said, trying to keep her talking.

She laughed. "Partly. But not the main part."

"What's the main part?"

"Business," she said. "Isn't that always the main part?"

"What business?"

"I'm slipping," she said, her voice a little vacant. "The fan mail is way off. Ratings are dropping. The producer doesn't return my agent's calls right away. The financing isn't coming through for my own studio. Are you getting the picture?"

"No, I don't get the picture," I said. "What has that got to do with this goddamn film?"

"And you call yourself a detective. You are a dense old man, Mr. Malory. I need a scandal. I need someone to blackmail me with this old footage. I need to go on Barbara Walter's and give a crying apology for what I did as a starving starlet. It'll be worth millions in publicity. I'll be hotter than Fawn Hall and Jessica Hahn put together."

Maybe it was time for me to hang it up. The world was getting too strange. What this had all been about, the killing of Orin, the attempts on my life, was a woman determined to set herself up to be blackmailed so her career could get a boost. "What'd you kill Orin for, then?" I yelled. "Why didn't you tell him to blackmail you, if that's all you wanted?"

"The little worm was not a man to be trusted. Once he learned my real intention, he would be back for hush money or he would go to Confidential Magazine and tell them I had set it all up. The public doesn't like fake tears. I couldn't risk that. So, I killed the little toad as soon as I had the reel."

"And you set me up as your patsy for Orin's killing."

"You'll have to admit, it was a nice plan. But you do seem to have a way to squeeze yourself out of things."

"Then you tried to have me killed too. What was that all about?"

"You got greedy."

"I didn't want anything from you."

"Yes you did. You wanted to find me. You wanted to find out what was none of your business."

"How long do you plan to keep killing people?"

"You will be the last."

I felt along the wall behind me for some access to the projection room. "You must never have played Lady Mac Beth. You can't get the security you want by killing everyone who comes along."

"You're the last of the loose ends, Mr. Malory. As I said, a very difficult loose end. When I found out you somehow had left Victor a cinder inside his red truck, I decided it was time to take matters in my own hands. You know: want the job done right, do it yourself. You see, it'll be easy to explain why I had to shoot you. A down-and-out detective, an alcoholic who can't even make a living anymore. A beautiful and rich Hollywood movie star is recommended to him. The detective sees all her jewelry and learns about her living habits and finally breaks into her on a night all the staff is away. Actress surprises detective in the act and, bang-bang, detective gets shot. I will still be hysterical when they carry you out in the body bag. I will be aghast when I identify you as the very detective I had hired to protect me. When they investigate, I am sure they will find a clandestine trail from San Francisco to the studio where you stalked me. It will all be so very convincing, don't you think?"

I checked the hammer on the Colt, gripping as tightly as I could in my left hand. The two on the screen were hard at it on the single bed, the camera zooming in for anatomically dramatic close-ups. I pulled out a little from the wall. There was a second small window: it was black inside the projection room. That meant she could see me and I couldn't see her.

"Don't try and get out of the room, Mr. Malory. It's a clever design. From the push of a button a steel plate blocks out any light from the single window you so conveniently found. The steel door entrance door is heavily bolted also. This was the screening room built by an old silent screen star who wanted to be sure no one slipped out during her screenings."

I jumped into the aisle and fired off three quick rounds into the cone of light coming from the projector. I heard a pop and sizzle as the bulb imploded. I clutched my injured arm against my chest, ran down the aisle between the rows of seats, and tucked myself between two of the plush over-stuffed seats of the front row.☐

The room flooded with bright light. I looked up into the massive rococo chandelier in the center of the high ceiling. There were rapid muted *thunks*, then thuds into the heavily padded chairs. A small revolver with a silencer pulled back out of the shattered projection room window. I finished off the magazine at that opening, but my left hand wasn't steady, and the shots only kicked off plaster around it.

From the blank screen came the sounds of slapping flesh and grunts and groans.

Presuming she was reloading, I dropped the empty magazine out of the Colt with my good hand and set the gun on the chair in front of me and tried to slip in a fresh one, pushing too hard and sending the gun sliding off the chair seat into the aisle. I leaned to get it and she let loose with another volley, two of them catching my right shoulder, jerking my arm, and setting the bone back loose. I fought against the blackness and the pain as I grabbed up the Colt and rocked back behind the big chair.□

I looked at my shoulder, there were two small holes in the jacket, but I didn't think any bone had been hit.

Another volley pumped into the chair— stuffing and bits of fabric whizzing by my head.

When I'd been able to get the new magazine in place, I let off half of it into the chandelier. The room fell back into darkness, shards of glass raining to the floor.

There was more moaning from the blank

screen, both the man and the woman now. The revolver went off again, spitting rapid bursts of flames. But the flames were shooting upward and the sound of the bullets striking were coming from the ceiling. I lowered the Colt and waited. There was a metallic clatter. The sound from the projector dropped to a strained hum as the voices from the screen descended to a growling stop. The clatter of the projector stopped altogether.□

I slowly got up. One of the shots must have hit my left leg somewhere because when I took a step I fell against the armchair next to me. I straightened up and hobbled toward the projection room wall.

I felt for the opening of the window and brought the Colt up in my shaking left hand to manage a shot.

It rang hollow from wall to wall.□

Nothing.

I reached through the opening and felt around the interior wall and found switches. One of them lit the room inside.

In the harsh light of the single bare bulb, she didn't look pretty at all now with her tongue dangling out the side of her mouth and her face ashen. She looked a little like she could be Crazy Freddie's sister. Shell casings littered the floor and the air was a cloud of bluish gun smoke.

I reached back inside and tried more switches. One of them popped open a heavy steel door leading into the projection room.

I limped through the small doorway.

The bright red scarf that had tangled in the

projector sprocket was pulled so tight around her throat that I couldn't get her free.

I found scissors on the splicing table and cut through the taut silk. Her body flopped to the floor.

I dropped to the floor next to her.

The straining projector freed itself from the cut silk. The film chattering through again.

"Oh, do it to me! Do me hard!" She cried from thirty years ago.

She howled. "More! More! Don't ever stop! Gimme more! Gimme more!"

I smiled as I thought: so this is how it ends. It was all right. The world will go on as if I never existed. But, at the end, I was doing what I was meant to do. What more could be expected from an old, bemused, and crazed creature like me?□

The film ended with a scream of pleasure, then the motor and gears and sprockets fell to a contented hum. I looked down at the pool of blood forming at the end of my twisted and broken right arm. It didn't hurt so much anymore.

As I leaned my head back, for some crazy reason, I thought of Timmy, Rita's cat, and realized I had never met him, but in the strangeness of it all, I thought I heard him in the distance, a mellow meow. I let my eyes close. The meow changed to a baby's cry. Strange was all I thought.□

Then the baby's cry changed to a distant siren. Who knows, maybe somebody had heard all the shots.